WILD IRISH MOON

THE MYSTIC COVE SERIES
BOOK TWELVE

TRICIA O'MALLEY

LOVEWRITE PUBLISHING

WILD IRISH MOON
The Mystic Cove Series
Book Twelve

Editors: Jenny Sims; David Burness

"Follow your inner moonlight; Don't hide the madness."–
Allen Ginsberg

CHAPTER 1

*E*very one of her clients had canceled.

Iris Moon Dillon, known affectionately to the world as Moon, stared blankly at her computer screen while her brain scrambled to process what was happening. Never the best before her first cup of coffee in the morning, Iris struggled to focus as her fingers flew over the keyboard. Her phone buzzed again, causing her to look closer at the screen. Typically, Iris hated her phone and did her best to ignore it at all costs. She already had enough demands on her time with her tightly packed schedule. As one of the top psychic mediums in the United States, she'd learned long ago that if she didn't protect her time, others would take advantage of her. But now, as her spirit guides screamed in her ear that something was *very* wrong, she took notice of the alerts streaming across her phone's screen.

"What the hell is going on?" Iris pushed her reading glasses up into her hair and rubbed her eyes, forcing herself to focus for a moment. The way her gift worked, her spirit guides would speak directly in her mind, and they often tried to get her attention. She'd learned how to mute them when needed or bring them to the forefront when she was ready to listen to what they had to say. Now, before she even picked up her phone, she gave herself a moment to tune into the guides who had been a focal point in her life.

"We warned you he was bad." This came from Lara, one of her main spirit guides, who had been with her since she was little.

"We warned you. But you didn't want to listen," Ophelia, her second strongest guide, added.

Nobody liked hearing "I told you so," so, Iris decided to mute them and picked up her phone. She stared in shock at the text messages that flew by, each coming in faster than the last. At first, all she saw was a jumble of words and then they all surfaced together like one of those word cloud maps. *Fraud. Fake. Scam artist.* The words blurred as sweat beaded on her forehead and panic twisted low in her gut. The next message that came in was from her friend John with an order to click a link to a blog post. Her finger hovered over the phone for a second, knowing that when she clicked the link, her entire world would change. A part of her wanted to turn her phone off and go back to bed, pulling the pillow over her head to pretend the outside world didn't exist.

But as a thirty-year-old woman who largely made her way on her own in this world, Iris knew that no matter how much people wanted to run from reality or hide from their pasts, the universe had a way of beating people over the head until they learned whatever lessons they needed to learn. She suspected whatever she was about to read would be one massive life lesson for her. Which, frankly, was kind of annoying. She'd finally found herself on even ground with what she thought was a somewhat stable relationship, a successful business, and a happy, well *sometimes happy*, home.

"*Liar,*" Ophelia whispered in her ear, reading her thoughts.

"I'm ignoring you right now," Iris said out loud. And before she could stop herself, she clicked the link to be taken to an online gossip blog, which, *of course*, featured an unflattering photo of Iris. This particular photo had been taken several years ago when she'd been at a Renaissance Faire. She hadn't wanted to have a booth, but her boyfriend, Warren, had insisted this would be a good way for her to reach new clientele. She'd felt silly all dressed up in a costume that made her look like a serving wench on a pirate ship, but she'd gone along with what Warren had wanted. A recurring theme in their relationship.

Now, seeing herself in that ridiculous costume with the headline proclaiming that she was nothing but a fraud made her double over and clutch her stomach. Bile rose in her throat, and it took every ounce of willpower not to race for the bathroom and dry heave into the toilet.

Ignoring her buzzing phone, Iris clicked to the internet on her laptop and started searching the gossip websites. Her heart sank as she saw that the news had picked up the story. It was no longer just one or two random influencers or gossip blogs claiming that she was a fraud. Mainstream sites like Woman Today Magazine and Listen Now! were running the story as well. In the past few years, her celebrity status had grown after she'd given a very successful reading to one of the top emerging musicians in the industry, Sirena. When Sirena had splashed the contents of the reading across her Instagram, Iris's business had exploded. Now, Iris had almost a year-long waiting list for clients to book a session. Which is why, when the cancelations poured in that morning, Iris knew her life was about to be irrevocably changed forever.

She picked up her phone and placed a call to Warren, her boyfriend and business partner. When the call went to voicemail, her spirit guides screamed in her ear. Ignoring them, she texted Warren, hoping he could offer some clarity on what had happened. They would have to issue a denial and perhaps get an attorney involved in order to fight these egregious claims. Tears threatened, as Iris's reputation in the business was everything to her. She'd been climbing her way up for her whole life, trying to eke out some semblance of an existence that would leave her in a safe space. Her gaze caught Warren's name in the article on the screen in front of her, and she narrowed her eyes as she leaned in.

"Warren Smith, Iris Moon's boyfriend and business partner, has finally come clean about how the psychic has spent the past few years defrauding vulnerable clients," Iris read out loud, horror filling her. "'I couldn't bring myself to support her anymore. Not when I knew that good people were getting hurt.'"

Iris's mouth dropped open, and she slammed her laptop shut, shoving back from her desk. Sweat ran down the back of her neck and beneath the faded sweatshirt she wore. Heart hammering in her chest, she began to pace her shop, unsure of how to proceed or what to do. Unbidden, a memory from high school arose, and Iris dropped to the floor and clutched her arms around her stomach as tears finally spilled over onto her cheeks.

She'd been fifteen years old, the awkward kid with the single New Age hippie mom, who dressed in thrift store clothes. That day, she'd been holed up with the theater kids in the auditorium, their frenetic energy and outlandishness helping with Iris's own shyness and awkward social skills. At that time, she'd finally realized what the voices in her head were trying to tell her, and once she'd understood she wasn't crazy and that the voices were just her spirit guides, she'd been ecstatic to share this newfound information with her group of friends. She'd been *so* excited to tell everyone, and Charlie, the lead in the play, had asked her to read him. When she'd mentioned his parents were about to get a divorce and that he would need to protect himself from their fighting, he jumped up and called her a freak. The rest of the students had followed his lead, laughing her off the stage, and she'd never hung out with them again. It was the first in a long line of experiences when she'd learn that many people did not like her peering into their vulnerable spaces.

Now, as her world crashed down around her, Iris was reduced from the confident woman she thought she'd become to a sniffling mess on the floor, no stronger than the insecure fifteen-year-old who had gone home that day and cried to her mother.

Iris jolted as a knock sounded on the front door of her shop. Gingerly, she pulled herself off the floor and tiptoed to the front door, nudging the tapestry curtain away from the window. Seeing her friend John's face on the other side brought tears to her eyes again, and she opened the door only to have him shove her back so fast that she gasped.

"Hurry!" John exclaimed. Rushing inside, he slammed the door and made sure the curtain was pulled tight over the window. Turning, he grabbed her by her shoulders and studied her carefully. "Sorry, doll, there were paparazzi outside your shop. If I had thought ahead, I would've dressed more nicely," John said. He looked down at his sweatpants and sneakers with a disgusted look on his face. Iris had to admit that this was positively sloppy for John, who was normally a fastidious dresser, which meant things had to be *really* bad.

"John, have you seen the news? I don't understand what's happened." Iris dashed the tears from her eyes. "How can Warren claim that I'm a fraud? He's the one who's been lying to people. I've been covering his tracks for a long time."

"Don't I know it? I've tried to tell you to stop cleaning up after his messes." John grabbed her arm and dragged her over to her sitting area. He was one of the few friends who had stayed by her side since high school, and she valued his opinion more than most.

"Don't you see what's happened?" John asked. "Warren's thrown you under the bus. He probably realized that you were close to getting rid of him and knew that his free ride was about to end. And you know what? You can make a lot of money selling stories to these gossip magazines."

"You don't think he actually sold a story, do you?" Iris looked at John, her mouth gaping open in shock. "Even he couldn't be that money hungry, could he?"

"Oh my dear, dear friend, how I love you. You always want to believe the best in people, don't you? I don't know how you've managed to ignore how awful Warren has been for all these years, but he was only using you. In fact, please tell me that you took my advice about your bank accounts." John reached over and grabbed her arms, his fingers digging into her soft flesh. "Did you make a separate account like I asked you to do?"

John was a financial planner, and he'd been hounding her for years not to be foolish with her money now that she was finally making boatloads of it. After watching her mother struggle growing up, Iris had listened, and she'd carefully put her money into various managed portfolios and separate bank accounts from her business. While Warren did have access to her business accounts, he did not have access to her private accounts, and she'd faithfully moved money each month. Still, the business account had a good sum of money in it, and she hated to lose any of it. Fear gripped her, and she shot up from the couch and raced over to her laptop to sign in to her online bank. John, right at her side, leaned over her shoulder as she signed in.

"Please tell me you didn't have a lot of money in the business account," John said as they stared at the now empty bank balance on her business statement.

"I kept around twenty thousand in the business bank account. I always moved the money like you said. I had it on an automatic transfer that Warren didn't have approval to touch. But that means he still got the twenty thousand if I'm to assume he took it." Iris's heart fell as she clicked through the recent transactions and saw that, indeed, just that morning, the money had been transferred to Warren's private account.

"Honey, you have to check your personal accounts just to ensure he didn't find your passwords anywhere." John's voice was deadly serious, and Iris knew he would go to battle for her if they found that Warren had stolen the rest of her money. They both held their breath as Iris signed into her personal accounts, and she sighed in relief when she saw everything looked to be in order. Signing out once more, Iris closed her computer and pushed it across the table. Turning, she looked up at John, grief ravaging her. "John, what do I do?"

"Well, first of all, honey, we are going to hire a publicist who deals with these kinds of things. PR agencies all over the world are used to handling far worse. And with that glance at your account, I can see you're well able to afford it. By the way? Can I tell you how proud I am of you for taking my advice and looking after your finances? At the very least, this should give you some breathing room while we figure out your next steps."

"A publicist? What in the world am I going to do with a publicist?" Iris asked, panic lacing her voice. "Don't you understand that I'm ruined? I have spent my whole life building myself up by my word and reputation alone. And in one fell swoop, that asshole has destroyed me. It doesn't matter whether it's true or not. People always seek to discredit psychics. And that's even when they have a good track record!" Iris threw up her hands. "Don't you see? It doesn't matter how much I try to fight this or what I try to do; this will *always* follow me now. The biggest magazines in the world are covering it. I'll have to change my name and start over somewhere or find an entirely new occupation. I don't even know what that would be or what that would look like." Iris began to breathe heavily as her panic took over.

John, knowing her, knelt at her feet and took her hands in his own. "Breathe with me. In. Out."

John led her through a series of breathing exercises their vocal coach had taught them in high school. Not that Iris had ever been a great singer, but she had tagged along to John's practices. Once he'd managed to talk her back from diving into a full-blown anxiety attack, he forced her to meet his eyes.

"Now I want you to listen to yourself. Or ask your spirit guides or whatever it is you need to do, but I'm going to ask you a question, okay?" John waited until Iris nodded.

"What do *you* want to do?" John asked, carefully enunciating each word.

Before he'd even finished speaking, the answer had already popped into her mind.

Perhaps the answer had been there all along,

"I want to go to Ireland," Iris said.

CHAPTER 2

"Kane, this is WorldFlix. You can't mess around with this deal. This is literally the biggest thing that will *ever* happen to your career," Grant Ellison, Kane's New York agent, shouted over the blare of city traffic.

Kane Wallace, known to the world as K.L. Wallace, author of the best-selling Rock Rebels books, had recently signed a deal with WorldFlix to produce an off shoot of the series that would follow the main character's son.

"Sure and I understand that this is a big deal. However, I'm just having a bit of a hard time right now," Kane said. He pinched the bridge of his nose with his two fingers and stared out the window at the bleary gray clouds that hung over the busy London street below him. He'd spent so many years scrambling for visibility and trying to prove himself as a writer. Now, when success of a level that he couldn't even comprehend knocked at his door, he'd found himself virtually unable to write.

"But do you even understand how huge this is? World-

Flix doesn't usually do this. Usually, they wait to see how successful a book is, and *then* they snap the rights up. The fact that they've bought not only this book but also the entire series before you've even written it is virtually unheard of, Kane," Grant exclaimed. He cursed at someone, and Kane could just imagine him shoving his way through the crowds of New York, ruthless and efficient as always.

"Sure, and I understand what a huge compliment that is. But you know I'm having a hard time. It's just that since Bean passed away, I've been, I don't know, man. It's just been rough, okay?" Bean, his adorable mutt of a dog, had died of old age nearly three months after his bride Alison had left him at the altar. If Kane was being honest, which he generally tried to be, the loss of Bean hurt more than the loss of Alison.

"Listen, you've got to get over Alison. She wasn't the right one for you. We could all see that. Now, what she did was shitty, I'll admit. No man deserves to be left at the altar. Particularly a nice guy like yourself. But you have to keep your eyes forward. There will be someone else out there for you," Grant said. It was the closest that Kane had ever heard him to being empathetic, which meant that he was well and truly concerned about Kane's ability to deliver this manuscript.

"I'm also upset about my dog if you remember, Grant." Sadness filled him as he thought about Bean's adorable face, and though he knew he'd given Bean an awesome life, the loss still stung. It was the worst part about having animals, Kane had learned. You don't get to keep them with you forever. By some cruel trick of fate, it just happened that he'd lost the two most steadfast things in his life roughly around the same time. He had to admit that his creativity had all but dried up after that, and he'd spent a lot of time walking the streets of London questioning what he would do with his life. Which was silly, really. Because he already knew what he wanted to do with his life. He was an author. He loved delving into fantasy worlds and building new and exciting stories for his readers to explore. When he'd first come up with the concept for his new book, a romantic comedy following the son of rock star King Rebel, he had been so excited about it that it had taken every ounce of his willpower to pay attention to his wedding plans and not immediately get started writing the book. Now he wondered if he should have focused more on his own path and less on trying to make Alison's perfect wedding dreams come true. A fact that stung more when he'd learned she'd been sleeping with his editor.

"Oh man, Bean was one of the best dogs. I hate everybody, and that includes you most of the time, but I *love* dogs. You know I was just as torn up about Bean as you were." And despite Grant's insult, Kane's mouth quirked in a smile. Sure, Grant could be a jerk, but he was an honest one at that. And when Bean died, Grant flew to London and spent the weekend getting Kane drunk and making sure he ate. He was a rough-around-the-edges tough New York agent, but somewhere very, *very* deep inside his chest beat a somewhat warm heart. It was one of the few reasons that Kane kept him on as an agent.

"I don't know if I will ever come to terms with losing Bean but, at the very least, I know I gave him a good life and made him happy. I guess I can't say the same for Alison, and maybe that's the kicker of it."

"Or maybe she was never yours to make happy, to begin with. It sounded like she was sleeping with your editor all along, so maybe she just wasn't the type of woman who could be pleased by one man. Hell, what do I know? I've gone through four divorces already." Grant barked out a laugh, and another horn blared in the background.

Kane watched as the gray clouds opened up, unloading a sheet of rain on the people below who scrambled into shops to avoid getting wet. "I'll admit I don't know when I've ever had a greater shock. She just seemed so *nice* to me. She was the ultimate people-pleaser, wasn't she? Alison was the girl next door, the one who was always so sweet to me and always willing to entertain my silly ideas or last-minute plans. I *thought* she was happy with me. I *thought* she understood when I got lost in my writing for days at a time and barely came up for air. And now I realize that was all a lie," Kane said. That part probably stung the most. He'd so severely misjudged Alison that he doubted his own ability to trust his instincts. That insecurity had then trickled from his broken relationship and now stained his career, his writing, and his idea for his new book. What if the new book was based on a really stupid premise? If WorldFlix had purchased the rights to his Rock Rebels series, at least he could tell himself that they knew what they were getting and that the fans already loved those books. But instead, WorldFlix had bought the rights to something he hadn't yet created. That in itself was entirely terrifying.

"Maybe you just need to get laid. Have you put your-self on the market at all? Do they have Tinder in London? Why don't you go on Tinder and hook up with a few girls and get her out of your system?" Grant asked.

"I wish it was that easy. Honestly? I don't even think I need to get her out of my system when it comes to having sex or being in a relationship. It's just the fact that I doubt myself now. I doubt everything I'm doing. In fact, I doubt why I'm even in London. You know what, Grant? I don't even *like* London. What am I even doing here?" Kane's voice rose as he continued to watch the rain piss down on the dirty street below him.

"Man, do you need me to come over there? You don't sound good. I thought you loved London. Isn't that why you live there?" Grant asked.

"No. I live here because Alison wanted to be near all the shops and the shows and the fancy restaurants. She said coming from such a small town, it was her dream to live in the big city and experience all this. Well, you know what? I hate it. I hate waiting in traffic. I hate dirty streets. I hate having to wait in queues for my coffee in the morn-ing. I don't want to be around so many people anymore. I don't like it." Kane wasn't sure where this was coming from, but an image of his homeland surfaced in his brain. An Irishman always missed his home, didn't he? A vision of misty green fields and quaint villages appeared in his mind and stuck there like a stubborn burr in his sock. "I think I need to get out of here."

"All right, now you're beginning to scare me. Where are you going? You need to go somewhere with cell service. And somewhere you can work. I'm going to get on a plane. Do you think I need to come out there? I don't like this. Kane, talk to me," Grant said, worry lacing his voice.

"I think I need to go back to Ireland," Kane said, shaking his head as he marveled over the thought. When he'd left Ireland years ago, he thought he wouldn't return as nothing kept him there. His parents had moved to the United States ten years ago seeking new adventures, and he'd stayed behind to finish his schooling and follow his heart when writing his first few books. At the time, he'd fancied himself quite the authentic writer as he would wander the massive library at Trinity College and work late nights in the coffee shops around the university. In fact, speaking to girls about the book he was working on had even gotten him laid a few times. But it had taken many years—until he'd broken out with his tenth book— before he'd finally achieved financial success. By that time, he'd grown jaded enough with the realities of writing to be happy to move to another country when his girlfriend at the time, Alison, had gotten a job transfer for her work. Granted, London hadn't been a top choice for him, but he'd been looking for a change. Now he realized how much he missed the quiet of the coastal villages in Ireland, and the more he thought about it, the more the idea took hold.

"But you're going to work, right? You're not going to do something rash and disappear on me, are you? Wherever you go, you'll have internet, right?" Grant asked, nerves in his voice.

"Grant, I don't think I could shake you if I tried." Kane laughed. "But I think I need to do something. And maybe this is the answer. I am literally waking up every morning and sitting in front of a blank screen on my computer, slowly going mad. If I don't shake this up or do something to change this, my writer's block will get worse, and I'm never going to get you a manuscript."

"I thought you said there was no such thing as writer's block. That it was just writers being lazy," Grant said.

"Did I really say that? God, I'm such an asshole. I guess I didn't really understand about writers working their way through grief, okay? I retract any of those statements. I do have writer's block, at least when it comes to this manuscript. I could probably write you a space opera or a few murder mysteries, particularly ones where a runaway bride gets murdered. Is that something you want to sell?" Kane asked with a wry smile on his lips.

"God save me from all you insane creatives," Grant griped. "Listen, man, go to Ireland. I can arrange a flight for you. I can arrange someplace to stay. You just say the word, and I will set it up for you. If you think this is the change you need, then I am a hundred percent behind it. Just make sure you get your words in each day."

"I don't need you to arrange anything. I know exactly where I'm going to go. I think it's the one place I've always felt at peace."

"Where's that? And can I get a ticket there as well? I don't know if I've ever known a moment's peace since I came screaming out of my mother's womb." Grant laughed. "Not that I think I'd even know how to enjoy it. To me, that sounds terrifying."

"It's a little town on the west coast of Ireland called Grace's Cove. I've only been for a few days before. Alison and I took a long weekend there. And I remember I thought about that town for a long time after. That's where I want to go."

"You don't think it will remind you too much of Alison?" Grant asked.

"No. You know what reminds me of Alison, Grant? Sitting here in this apartment we used to share and staring at some of her clothes she still has yet to pick up. *That* reminds me of her," Kane said, pulling up a flight schedule on his laptop. "I'll let you know when I get in."

"All right, man. Safe travels, and try to get laid while you're there. It might do you some good."

"Do you want me to get laid, or do you want me to write a book?" Kane asked.

"Scratch that. Write the book, then get laid. I'll check in with you soon."

CHAPTER 3

"What do you mean there are no cars?"

It had never once occurred to Iris that she'd need to book a car in advance. Airports always had rental cars available, didn't they? Now, as she stood at the almost empty counter of the car rental place in Shannon Airport, Iris stared at the clerk, who looked like a kindly grandfather. It was one more thing in a long line of mishaps, and Iris wondered if this would be the moment that finally sent her over the edge. She'd barely slept in the past three days. Between dyeing her hair, packing her bags, and dodging the paparazzi, Iris was certain she was careening toward a breakdown. True to his word, John had not only engaged the services of an entertainment attorney, but he'd also hired a PR firm, who had immediately jumped into action defending Iris's reputation. And while the magazines, well at least *some* of them, had printed her denial, a psychic fraud was a far juicier story than a vengeful now ex-boyfriend.

She still hadn't been able to get in touch with Warren,

but she'd changed the locks and her passwords. Before blocking him, she'd let him know just what she thought of him. John had suggested that she open a legal case against Warren. Though the thought of pursuing legal action against someone she had recently shared a bed with made her stomach turn, Iris had meekly followed John's advice. He had been her guiding star through this chaos. While Iris was typically capable of making decisions for herself, she realized that she must have been far closer to burnout and emotional overwhelm than she thought. Having John come in and essentially take control of the situation felt like her guardian angel had come down from the heavens and was lifting her up. Maybe her hand had shook a bit when she'd signed her statement and pressed criminal charges against Warren for stealing from her company, but she'd still signed her name, hadn't she? At that moment, she started gaining some of her strength back. Now, however, she looked at the smiling older gentleman who shrugged his shoulders sheepishly and tried to compute what was happening.

"Sure, and it's a sad thing, isn't it, miss? However, we have a huge festival going on right now, which is popular with a lot of Europe, and we've sold out of all our cars. Because we're a bit of a smaller airport, we don't have the same availability as a larger airport like Dublin. However, I can take a look and see what I can get for you at the end of this week or into next weekend?"

"Next weekend?" Iris stared blankly at the man. *Next weekend?* She didn't even know what she was going to do tomorrow, let alone next weekend. All she knew was that John had booked her a long-term rental accommodation in a town that was still quite a drive from the airport. Perhaps she could hire a taxi to take her there. However, based on the emptiness of the airport, she suspected that might be a long shot. "Um, I'm not sure if next weekend will work for me. I don't... I don't know what to do."

Iris realized she was dangerously close to tears and stepped back from the counter, not wanting to turn into a blubbering mess in front of other people. The man seemed to sense her distress, and his eyes softened.

"Sure, and if you'll be letting me just take care of this gentleman behind you, I can see what I can be doing to help you. Don't worry, we'll figure something out for you, okay?" Iris nodded her thanks, gripping her purse tightly in her hands, and moved aside. She spotted a little bench not far from the car rental counter and dragged her luggage over to it, plopping down onto the seat as she tried to get control of her emotions. She envied the man standing at the counter, looking carefree and well-organized. He probably didn't have any problems in his life, Iris thought, though she knew that wasn't likely. After reading hundreds of people over the years, she realized everybody had their own issues. However, the way he smiled confidently at the man behind the counter and was handed a car key in a matter of moments made Iris just a little bit jealous.

The man was well-dressed in the way of Europeans. Where she wore leggings, her purple boots, and an oversized sweatshirt topped with her leather jacket, this man had on a checked suit coat thrown over an old band T-shirt with fitted denim pants and nice boots. He looked casually cool and confident, and when he turned, a smile still on his face, Iris's breath caught. He was also ridiculously handsome, she realized. He was good-looking in a polished sort of way, with dancing blue eyes, thick brown hair, and an easy air of seeming to know his space in the world. Iris always admired people who carried themselves in such a way. It was as though they were comfortable in the fact that they belonged here and were *allowed* to take up space. Iris had spent a long time fighting to prove her worth, both to the skeptics and to herself, when she should have just been claiming her space instead.

Warren had done that to her. He'd always wanted to be famous. However, he'd never had any real talent in their industry. Before she could go down the dark hole of beating herself up about Warren, Iris realized that the man she was currently ogling was walking directly toward her. Her eyes widened when he stopped in front of the bench and gave her a smile that eradicated all thoughts of her ex-boyfriend and made her want to step into this man's arms. This was such an unnatural reaction for Iris that she shrank back into her seat. The man, catching her reaction, lifted both hands in the air as though to say he meant no harm.

"I couldn't help but overhear your predicament and thought I would ask where you were headed?" He smiled easily at her, the whisper of Ireland in his accent. "I thought perhaps I could be giving you a ride if we were heading the same way?"

"You want to give me a ride?" As soon as she said it, Iris realized that her tone had sounded far more suggestive than she'd meant to imply, and immediately, her face flushed. "Um, I'm going to a town called Grace's Cove. Do you know it?"

"Sure, and that's lucky for us both, isn't it? I'm headed

there meself, and I'd be more than happy to have you join me on the drive and drop you at your accommodation. My name's Kane, by the way." Kane smiled at her again, and Iris was instantly put on alert.

"My mother warned me about accepting rides from strangers." Iris narrowed her eyes at him, not liking how quickly he'd charmed her. Warren had also been charismatic, and now she tuned into her spirit guides to see if they had something to say about this far too handsome man offering to give her a ride.

"He's safe," Ophelia whispered in her mind. *"I promise you he's safe. You need someone safe. Go with him."*

One of the things bothering Iris over the past few days between trying not to read all the articles being written about her was that she'd so roundly ignored her spirit guides when it came to Warren. They had warned her for years about him, and she'd brushed their advice aside, like a rebellious teenager not wanting to listen to her mother's words of caution. Now, she realized that it had been stupid of her to do so. Here she was, relying on spirit guides to help her clients on their various paths, yet when it came to her own life, she'd ignored their words of wisdom. She'd promised herself moving forward that she would stop being her own worst enemy and *actually* listen to her guides because she had a tool in her tool belt that most people didn't. So even though it went against what she'd been taught, Iris decided to take the ride. Not only was she exhausted but she also wanted to get out of a somewhat public space in case someone recognized her. She couldn't be certain that the news hadn't been picked up internationally, and though she'd since dyed the purple out of her hair and now sported auburn locks, there was still a slight chance she could be spotted.

"Is it a habit of yours to offer rides to strange women in airports?" Iris arched an eyebrow at Kane.

"Oh sure, I do it every weekend. That's how I pick my victims." Kane smiled at her again, and when Iris narrowed her eyes, he burst out laughing. "No, it's not the usual for me. However, it's hard for me to resist a damsel in distress. And since we're both headed the same way, I don't mind sharing my car with you. I don't know what help I can be once we're in Grace's Cove. However, from what I remember of the town, you should be able to get around on foot just fine. Of course, it depends where you've rented your accommodation, but if you're right in town, you'll be able to walk to shops and restaurants and should be just fine on foot until you figure out what to do about your car."

"Oh, you've been before? I guess that makes me feel a little bit better. I will accept your offer of a ride," Iris said and stood. She held out her hand. "My name is Iris, and I thank you for your assistance." When Kane took her hand, a jolt ran up her arm, and warmth flooded her body. She caught, for a moment, on his eyes, and saw that he, too, felt something. They dropped their hands, quickly stepping away from each other, and Kane cleared his throat.

"The car park's this way. I don't think we'll have trouble finding which one's ours," Kane joked, breaking the moment.

They trundled their suitcases out of the airport and across the empty lot to where a midsize car sat in the very last space. Iris was happy she hadn't packed more because she was certain the car wouldn't have fit more than their two suitcases. Once they were on the road, Iris became immediately grateful that she had listened to her spirit guides. She'd forgotten about driving on the other side of the road, not to mention a stick shift, as well as having to navigate. Her stomach twisted as Kane shot around a corner with a cheerful beep of the horn and zipped along a narrow road. Iris was certain they would take out a wall at any moment.

"So, Iris, what brings you to my lovely country? You're American, right?" Kane asked.

"A bad breakup," Iris said, surprised that tidbit had jumped out of her mouth. It was highly unusual for her to share personal details of her life, as she was always focused on listening to other people's problems. Now, as they careened toward certain death on the windiest, most narrow road she'd ever been on in her life, Iris figured, what did it matter? They'd be dead within the hour at this rate anyway. "I've had a bit of a hiccup in my life, I guess you'd say. And my ex-boyfriend betrayed me. For some reason, I seemed to think that hopping on a plane to Ireland was what I needed."

"Is that right? Well, Iris, in the nature of comradery and good will, I can tell you that I am here for much the same reason. I *also* had a bad breakup." Kane gave her a sympathetic look, and Iris vacillated between warming to him and wanting to scream at him to keep his eyes on the road.

"So it's the broken hearts club, huh?" Iris asked. "Do you want to talk about it?"

"Is this a game of I'll show you mine if you show me yours?" Kane laughed at Iris's look. "I meant telling me your story. Although if you do want to show me anything else, I might be game for it."

To her absolute shock, Iris realized that Kane was lightly flirting with her. It had been years since she had been in any sort of social situation where someone would flirt with her and, even then, it was a rare occurrence. Perhaps it was her bristly nature, or her wild-colored hair, or the fact that she was naturally distrustful of most people, but Iris had long ago understood that she wasn't the type of woman who got hit on.

"Eyes on the road, buddy. I've got no goods to offer," Iris said, though warmth slipped through her at the thought that this delicious man might actually want to get in bed with her.

"I beg to differ, but since I don't want to be the creep who makes the lone woman I've picked up in my car uncomfortable, I will instead tell you great tales of my heartbreak. Nothing woos a woman more than hearing about how another woman has stomped all over a man's heart, right?"

"Well, we are a bloodthirsty lot," Iris said and was pleased when Kane laughed.

"Don't I know it? Allow me to weave you a classic brokenhearted tale of unrequited love," Kane said. While his tone was light, Iris noticed that his knuckles had turned white as he gripped the steering wheel. Whatever he was about to tell her still hurt for him. Despite not wanting to get involved, Iris could already feel herself wanting to make it better for him. "In a classic runaway bride story, my bride left me at the altar. It turns out that she had been sleeping with my ... " At his pause, Iris glanced at Kane to see his lips pressed together in a tight line. It was as though he'd been about to say something and caught himself in time. Iris could understand that, as she would also have to give a redacted version of her own story. Allowing him the time to collect himself, she stared out the window at rolling green fields dotted with little white fluff balls of sheep.

"She was sleeping with a colleague of mine," Kane finally continued. "For years. And all that time, not once had I suspected anything. I think that is what shook me more than anything. She was so sweet and kind and what I thought was an easygoing fit into my life. And the whole time, she'd been lying to me. I guess my biggest issue is what does that say about me if I can't even notice that the person I thought I loved was lying to me?"

"It means that you want to believe the best of people. And that you're willing to trust until that trust is broken. It's not a bad trait," Iris said. She took her eyes off the sheep to study Kane's striking visage once again. "You can't beat yourself up for information you didn't have."

Now if she could only give herself the same advice, Iris thought. However, she *had* been privy to information in a way that others weren't. Her spirit guides warned her away from Warren. She should have known better. Kane, on the other hand, had acted on good faith in his relationship.

"You say that so easily. I wish I could believe it. Instead, it feels like my entire life has been thrown into question. Because if I didn't catch that she was a liar and a cheat, what else am I missing? How can I trust anything?" Kane laughed ruefully. "I suppose that's getting a little deep for having just met you. Anyhow, that's my side of things. What about you?"

"Much the same," Iris said, "except there wasn't any cheating. That I know of, at least. We were business partners, and he betrayed me and stole my money." It was about as much as Iris was willing to share without giving away too many details. She wasn't ready to give more information until she had a better idea if anyone overseas had heard of her plight.

"Well, now that's just shite, isn't it? You're supposed to be able to trust the people you're in business with. And for him to steal from you? I hope you filed charges." Kane's brow wrinkled in anger for her, and Iris found that she could smile.

"I *did* file charges. In fact, I think that was the only moment in all of this that I actually felt like I was taking some of my power back." At her words, Kane looked at her in surprise.

"Taking your power back. That's such an interesting way to phrase it. Maybe that's something I really need to think about."

For the rest of the ride, as though they'd reached an unspoken agreement that they had both danced too close to vulnerable spaces, they spoke of nonsense things like sports, weather, and their favorite foods. By the time they crested the hill and drove into Grace's Cove, Iris was all but drooping from exhaustion. However, she was grateful she had listened to her spirit guides. Kane had proved to be a witty and intelligent distraction, and she was more than delighted that they'd arrived at their destination in one piece.

The village of Grace's Cove spread out before her, and something shifted inside Iris, like a key fitting into a lock. Colorful houses dotted rolling green hills that hugged a softly curved harbor. On the water, a few ships sailed home for the night, and Iris wondered if they were fishing or tour boats. As they drove farther into the village, the buildings mashed more closely together, and each sported a brightly colored door. Altogether, Iris found herself charmed, and a soft sigh of pleasure escaped her lips.

"It gets you, doesn't it? I've only been here once but, still, this place has called to me. I'm glad to be back," Kane said as he pulled to a stop in front of Iris's accommodation. Turning, he held out a hand. "Gallagher's Pub is right down the street and has the best meal in town. I'll be there for a pint later if you're feeling sociable."

Iris took his hand, feeling that same jolt of recognition run up her arm, and her realization that she wanted to see Kane again unsettled her.

"I likely won't be," Iris answered, forgetting to be polite.

"At least I know you're being honest with me." Kane laughed. "Until I see you next then, Iris."

CHAPTER 4

$\mathcal{T}$he cottage was exactly what Kane had hoped for when he'd called the rental agency, equally as charming as it was serviceable. He'd happily signed a six-month lease, not caring if Grant would freak out that he was going off grid or not. London didn't make him happy. While Kane wasn't sure what did make him happy these days, that much he did know.

Located farther up the main hill behind Grace's Cove, the cottage had a bird's-eye view of the village and the harbor but still allowed for a comfortable walk into town when he fancied a pint and some conversation. However, the cottage also came with the welcome benefit of being situated on several acres of its own land, rendering the nearest neighbor a good ten-minute walk away. Truly, the combination of privacy along with the opportunity to socialize, if needed, made Kane's introverted heart sing.

The cottage setup was fairly simple, with the front door leading directly into the combined kitchen and living area. There, a low-slung leather couch was situated in front of a lovely fireplace. A cozy armchair in the corner faced the long row of windows that looked out to the water. On either end of the main room, two doors led to small but respectable bedrooms, both sporting tiny en suite bathrooms. He already knew which bedroom he'd use for his office and made a mental note about getting a desk delivered after the weekend. In the meantime, he'd work just fine at the small dining room table tucked in a corner across from the kitchen. Long wooden beams crossed the ceiling, and the stone walls were painted a soft white. Vibrant rugs were tossed across the wood floor, adding warmth to the room, and a basket of throw blankets was tucked by the sofa. Kane walked to the French doors in the kitchen, and his heart did a little dance. Unlocking the door, he pushed it open and stepped into the cool early evening air.

As far as the eye could see, nature beckoned. No buildings, no stores, and no endless line of cars. Instead, several chairs had been tucked around a table and a small firepit with fairy lights strung above. Beyond that, the hills rolled away in an endless swath of green that brought a smile to Kane's lips. He'd missed Ireland.

Without thinking twice, Kane bent and untied his boots, removing them along with his socks. Then he strode across the backyard and into the field, a shiver running through him as his feet dug into the damp earth. Smiling, he turned and faced the water, allowing himself to take the first real deep breath he'd taken in months. A touch of the sea mixed with wet earth filled his nostrils, and Kane reveled in how much he'd missed this connection to nature. What had he been doing locking himself up in that tiny apartment in London when he could have acres of land to wander here? This was exactly what he'd needed.

Kane continued to walk, stepping carefully so as not to hurt himself, enjoying the squish of mud between his toes. This felt like taking his power back, the term Iris had used popping into his head. This...this felt like the start of the path he needed to be on to right his ship, so to speak.

Thinking of Iris brought her face to his mind. He paused, an amused smile on his lips as he thought about her mismatched features. She was all angles and sharp lines mixed with soft lips and almond-shaped eyes. Nothing about her face should have gone together. It was like someone had mixed two different puzzles in the same box, yet Kane had found it difficult to look away from her. How she'd rapid-fire her thoughts on damn near anything yet immediately shut down when he danced too close to any serious topic was fascinating. Her face lit when she spoke of something she liked, her hands moving in the air so fast it was almost like she was acting out her words while her shock of auburn hair tumbled around her head. The red wasn't real, as Kane had been able to see the faint line of dye on her forehead, but he found the color high-lighted the misty gray-green of her cat-like eyes.

She was running from something, of that much he was sure. As an observer of people, Kane picked up on nuances that others might not. And Iris had instantly reminded him of a wounded animal, suspicious of the outside world and bristly when approached. Though he was certain a thera-pist would have something more to say about it, her vulnerability coated in armor spoke to the hero complex inside him. Although Kane wasn't sure if it was a complex so much as an ego thing. Most men he knew had daydreams of being a hero in one scenario or another. It was why he wrote books, after all. If he couldn't be a hero in real life, at least he could create worlds where he lived out all those daydreams. The feeling of failure that had plagued him since Alison had left him at the altar filled him once more.

Instinctively, he knew that he'd dodged a bullet. Alison wasn't his soul mate, nor had it been the kind of love he wrote about in his stories. But at the same time, he'd grown comfortable with her, and she'd fitted neatly into his life. It was the sense of failure, though, that dogged him now. As a creative, he tended to be hard on himself and the work he produced. It didn't matter how many rave reviews he received. If he allowed himself to read the bad ones, he would remember those words. With Alison, it didn't matter how many times his friends had told him that she had been the one in the wrong or that it wasn't his fault. He still couldn't shake the feeling of defeat.

Plus, how was he supposed to write about love when he clearly knew nothing about it? Maybe that was the crux of his issue with his current manuscript. He was diving into new territory that he had been quite excited about when he'd pitched the concept. Now, he felt barefoot at the bottom of Mount Everest as he stared up at the unattainable peak.

A breeze kissed his cheeks, bringing with it the scent of the sea, and Kane inhaled deeply, nature settling the nerves that threatened to kick up. *This* felt right. Being here, at this moment, in this village that he'd often dreamed of, felt like the first step he'd made on the road to finding himself again. Kane returned to the cottage when his stomach rumbled, reminding him that he hadn't eaten since a hurried granola bar early that morning. Already, he felt calmer than he had in months.

Hopefully, Grace's Cove would work her magic on him.

CHAPTER 5

"That is so not like you," John's voice exclaimed through the phone as Iris unpacked her bag. The apartment she rented was small but serviceable, and Iris found the space cozy and welcoming. While some people would have cringed at the narrow bathroom and shared bedroom and living space, Iris warmed to it. She hadn't grown up with much and had lived well within her means for years now. Big houses and large spaces made her uncomfortable and increased her anxiety about having one more thing to take care of. With only one suitcase to unpack and her future uncertain, Iris appreciated the coziness of her quarters. A double bed was tucked neatly in a small alcove on one side of the room and made up with a thick woven quilt and plenty of plush pillows. At the foot of the bed sat an oversized loveseat in a soft turquoise material, and Iris imagined it would be a lovely spot to curl up with a book. Pretty curtains picked up the turquoise color in a brocade pattern and framed large windows that looked out over the busy harbor. Below, people wandered past on their way to dinner or clutching shopping bags from the market.

On the other side of the room, a small kitchenette was tucked next to the door, with a window that overlooked a walled courtyard that the residents could use. Iris wasn't much of a cook, but the kitchen more than suited her needs with a small cooktop, a kettle for tea, and a toaster oven. Since it looked like the market was close by, she'd be able to make do with the small cabinets, as she wasn't really a foodie anyway.

"I know," Iris said. She finished putting her clothes away in the armoire, the only storage piece of furniture in the room, and plopped down on the loveseat. "I surprised myself at that. But my spirit guides promised me he was safe, and you know I'm trying to be better about listening to them."

"Yes, but when I suggested you listen to them more, I wasn't advising taking long car rides with random strangers in a foreign country," John said.

"He was harmless. Plus, you know I like to give people the benefit of the doubt. I find that most people, given the chance, want to help you." Iris furrowed her brow as her thoughts drifted to Warren. The pain came, sharp in her gut, his betrayal still fresh.

"And that's what landed us in this mess, isn't it?" John chided her gently, and Iris shrugged a shoulder. He wasn't wrong.

"Thank you for taking care of me, John. You're..." Iris's voice caught as she thought about how lucky she was to have the type of friend who could wade into the middle of chaos and weather the storm with her.

"The best? Don't I know it." John laughed. "Plus, I got a date out of it."

"Who? How?"

"I guess wearing gray sweatpants at your doorstep was a good choice. Some pictures ran in the press somewhere, and I was labeled a thirst trap. A few guys slid into my DMs and, well, one seems actually nice, and we're going to dinner later."

"I love this so much." Iris cheered up immediately. "Like, seriously, I can't wait to hear all the details. Where are you going for dinner?"

"Suzette's. It's meant to be the talk of the town. They do a surprise menu," John said.

"Even cooler. Yay! I'm beyond delighted for you. And, as a woman, I'll admit, gray sweatpants on a guy is hot. It's just…yeah. Maybe we'll have some silver linings out of this whole mess after all." Iris sighed happily.

"You know, Iris…that's one of my favorite things about you. No matter that your world is falling apart, you still always rejoice in happiness. I've always thought that was your best quality. You, well and truly, want other people to be happy. It's what makes you so good at your job. I've gotten other readings, you know." John lowered his voice conspiratorially.

"You haven't!" Iris gasped, her hand on her chest. "You, too, have betrayed me!"

"Hey now, how am I supposed to understand your industry if I don't try out other services? At least then, when you told me what you were up against with getting people to trust you or what some of your challenges were, I could better understand," John explained. Iris could hear him running water in the background as he put on his tea.

"I'm not *actually* mad, John. It's always good to get other opinions. I can only catch so much in my readings. Perhaps others can do better," Iris said. She meant it, too. She certainly wasn't all-knowing.

"Well, I can tell you there are a lot of hacks out there. I could see when someone was trying to get information from me or lead my questions so they could give me the answers they thought I wanted. But you don't do that. You're the real deal. I'm going to make it my mission to exonerate your reputation. Oh, and to squash Warren like the cockroach he is. I've got some ideas there, as well."

"Have they found him?" Iris asked, pinching her nose. Someone laughed outside, the sound carrying through the slightly cracked window, and Iris wanted to be as carefree as the woman down below.

"Not that I've heard. He's probably on a plane to South America right now."

"Like he'd think that far ahead." Iris sighed. Warren hadn't been the brightest, which was another reason it stung that he'd pulled this stunt on her. Well, that and he'd singlehandedly ruined her reputation and destroyed her career. For a lousy twenty thousand dollars. If Iris had known he'd needed the money that badly, she would have given it to him simply to forego the mess she now found herself in. Some things were more important than money, and now Iris felt like a rudderless ship as she stared out at where the sun kissed the horizon.

"No, likely not. What did you see in that man again?"

"He chose me," Iris said, hating how it made her sound. But it was the truth. Warren had chosen her when others had not. It was a lesson her mother had drilled into her for years. Being lonely was worse than being alone. So Iris had settled, content to be a part of a couple, and had staunchly avoided any deep self-reflection. Now, it seemed she'd have nothing but time for introspection, the thought of which was not particularly appealing at the moment. At the very least, maybe she would go out tonight to get the lay of the land.

"Well, honey, next time, you do the choosing, okay?" John said. "I gotta run. Call me tomorrow. Don't do anything stupid."

"I won't. Keep me posted on the hot date. I can't wait to hear about it," Iris said and disconnected. At least she could still smile at the idea of love, Iris thought as she stood from the couch. Deciding to freshen up before she explored, Iris showered and put on a simple pair of dark jeans, a loose black sweater, and grabbed her leather jacket. Slipping on her purple boots, she made sure she had her key before bounding down the stairs and out into the cool early evening air. It was weird to step out onto the street with no destination, no agenda, and no...anybody to meet. Just her. On her own. Wandering. The concept was so foreign to Iris that she wondered how she would manage being on her own.

Perhaps she was closer to burnout than she'd realized. She'd been burning the candle at both ends for years, always saying yes to every opportunity that came her way, and now she, quite literally, had nothing to do. The concept was so unusual for her that she stood outside the apartment building for several minutes, unsure where to go. Finally, realizing she might look a little ridiculous, Iris abruptly turned left and began to walk toward the water.

Her apartment building was located about midway up a hill, and houses and shops clustered together along the street that curved gently toward the harbor. The sun was just setting, casting a warm glow across the buildings, and some of the tension that gripped Iris's shoulders eased. Nobody gave her a second look, which meant that she likely looked like just another tourist and Iris soon found herself caught up in window-shopping. She passed a pottery shop, a bakery, a textile shop, and several galleries. At one such gallery, Iris paused, seeing that the sign was still flipped to open. On impulse, she stepped inside and was immediately welcomed by the soft cedar and vanilla scent, along with gentle folk music playing over the speakers. Charmed, Iris walked to a row of photographs and smiled at one where an old man with a newsboy cap laughed in a pub. She wanted to feel the same way this picture did—carefree, relaxed, and among friends. Iris instinctively understood that whoever took the photo of this man did so with love.

"That's our Mr. Murphy. He's a national treasure, that one."

Iris looked up at the voice, her eyes widening as a stunning older woman walked across the shop, nodding at the print.

"He lives here?" Iris asked, realizing the question was a bit silly, but her mind was working on overdrive to filter through the impressions she was getting from this woman.

A hint of otherness about her made Iris want to tune into her spirit guides.

"He does at that. His whole life. You'll likely see him if you head to Gallagher's Pub for a pint at all. Are you staying here for a while?" The woman studied her with the same open assessment. It was like two footballers meeting on the pitch and neither stepping forward to challenge the other. Not that Iris was in the nature of challenging other psychics, but she did like to acknowledge when someone else dealt in the mystical like she did.

"I might be. I'm undecided at the moment," Iris said, noncommittal as she continued to stroll the room, tuning into Lara, who was trying to get her attention. "These are lovely paintings."

"Yes, that's our resident artist, Aislinn. She's quite famous for her paintings. Her use of light and colors reflects her depiction of auras or the moods she sees around nature. I'm Morgan, by the way, and I manage Aislinn's works."

"You need to speak to her," Lara whispered in her mind. *"She has knowledge to help you."*

Since Iris couldn't exactly respond to Lara, she put her mental shields back up. That was the danger of having the ability to speak to spirits in her head. She often looked weird when she muttered to herself.

"That's fascinating. Does she actually see auras, or is it just what she thinks they might look like?" Iris stopped in front of a particularly moody painting done in virulent reds and oranges with a deep burgundy streak through the middle. The violence mimicked much of the feelings that Iris had been going through that week. Not that she would buy this piece—it was too turbulent and unsettled for her —but she appreciated the honesty of the work. Something was to be said for artists who could depict all ranges of emotions, even the unsettling ones.

"You'll have to ask her yourself," Morgan demurred, standing next to Iris and looking down at the painting. "She was in a mood when she painted this one."

"I can see that." Iris laughed, glancing at Morgan and appreciating the lightness dancing in the pretty woman's eyes. "I was just thinking what a skill she has to be able to translate such unsettling moods onto the canvas."

"Her lighter ones sell better unless it is a seascape. I do find a moody ocean print often appeals to our clientele." Morgan crossed the room and gestured to a wall full of paintings of the harbor at Grace's Cove, as well as others of an empty beach. Iris was drawn to those. She stopped in front of one, in particular, her breath catching, and she knew instantly this painting was meant for her.

The sun was just setting over the darkened waters of the cove, golden rays streaking across the deep blue surface like a benediction. Craggy rock walls hugged the beach, cocooning it in privacy while waves churned around a cluster of rocks. Or were they rocks? Iris leaned closer and realized that the rocks could almost suggest the form of a person. It was as though someone had walked into the water and the finality and beauty of it caused Iris's heart to skip a beat. Her hands trembled, and she clenched her fists tightly to avoid tearing the painting from the wall.

"I'd like to purchase this piece," Iris said with certainty in her voice.

"It's called *The Beginning*," Morgan murmured, and

Iris turned to meet her eyes. An understanding passed between them, but Iris wasn't yet ready to explore what that meant. She was tired from travel, hungry, and more than a little untethered. There would be time to speak with this woman further if needed.

"I think it's meant for me," Iris said, not filtering her thoughts, and Morgan's eyes widened slightly. She glanced down at the slim watch she wore on her wrist.

"It's actually past our closing time, and our tills are closed. I'll be happy to wrap it for you, and you can come back tomorrow? Or did you want to take it with you now?"

"You'd let me take it without paying for it?" Iris tilted her head in question at Morgan.

"Yes, I believe you to be trustworthy," Morgan said, shrugging one shoulder.

So she had been measuring Iris. There was more to unpack here, but Iris knew she'd have to do so at another time.

"I'll come back for it. I think I'm going to go to this Gallagher's Pub I've heard about and get some dinner, and then I plan to fall face-first into my bed and sleep for sixteen hours. You'll hold the painting for me, if you don't mind?"

"I will, of course. We also have prints of it. I haven't mentioned the price, but here's the information. It's quite a lot, dear, so I can also have a print framed for you if you prefer a more economical version," Morgan said politely, slipping a small card from a little cardholder beneath the painting. Iris didn't even glance at the price.

Which, truth be told, was probably one of the boldest and most out-of-character things she'd ever done. Aside from hopping on a plane to Ireland with no direction or real destination in mind, that is. But for someone who had spent a huge amount of her life counting pennies, not to even glance at the price tag on the painting was, well, it was kind of insane.

In a good way, Iris realized, as little bubbles of exhilaration rose inside her. Perhaps she was a little giddy from the week, but this choice felt right. The painting was meant for her, and because Iris had been so careful with her money, it didn't hurt for her to splurge on occasion.

"Thank you, but I'd like the original. It's a masterpiece," Iris said. Pride filled her, like someone settling a warm velvet cape over her shoulders, and she lifted her chin. She was buying this painting. With her own money, which she'd worked really hard for. If this was the first step in finding her feet again, it felt right. She'd just have to make sure this new spending habit didn't leak over into many frivolous things, but Iris sincerely doubted it would.

"I think you're right. This painting is meant for you." Morgan reached up and lifted it from the wall, carrying it across the room and through a doorway into another room. Iris didn't follow, instead feeling a bit bereft at the empty spot that now filled the wall in front of her. "Luckily, she's recently completed a new one that's the same size."

Iris turned as Morgan returned with another painting in her arms and carefully hung it in the empty space on the wall. This painting was of the harbor at moonlight, the pale light reflecting off the water and a few colorful fishing boats tucked in for the night. It was equally as beautiful, skill-wise, but didn't carry the emotional punch of the last painting.

"She's quite talented."

"You can meet her tomorrow when you come pick up your painting. I'll just take down your information?" Morgan held up a pad of paper. Iris hesitated and then wrote her information. She left Moon out of her name, only writing it as Iris Dillon.

"Dillon?" Morgan asked, tapping a finger against her lips, and Iris stilled, waiting for the woman to recognize her. "Are you Irish, then? There are a few with that surname in the village."

"Are there really?" Iris let out a small sigh of relief. Nothing to do with tabloid stories and merely an Irish woman being friendly. "Not that I know of, but you never know. Us Americans tend to be mutts."

"Yes, you do at that," Morgan murmured and then brightened. "Enjoy Gallagher's Pub. Tell Cait to put a pint on our tab for you. It's the least we can do after such a lovely purchase you've made."

"Oh, you don't have to…" Iris protested as Morgan ushered her to the door, seeming to be in a hurry now.

"I insist. Just ask for Cait. Tell her Morgan sent you, and she'll set you up nicely. Have a lovely evening, Iris. We'll be seeing you in the morning, then."

With that, Morgan closed the door neatly, and Iris found herself amused at the woman's brisk closure. She couldn't fault Morgan. Iris often found herself in the position of having a client desperate to continue speaking with her, and she'd had to wrap things up succinctly a time or two herself.

Feeling proud of herself for making her first real adult

splurge, Iris hummed her way up to Gallagher's Pub and swung through the cheerful front door.

It wasn't until her eyes landed on Kane's smiling face that she realized she'd completely forgotten about the man who'd asked her to dinner that night.

CHAPTER 6

$\mathcal{K}$ane caught Iris's look of surprise and then resignation when her gaze landed on him. He bit back a smile and shifted at the table, making a show of clearing space for her. Not that he'd force the woman to have dinner with him, but he hoped she'd join him. He'd enjoyed their conversation earlier that day, and she'd managed to stick in his head since. Now, he wanted to peel back the layers and see if he could figure out what she was running from. Perhaps it wasn't his greatest character trait, this endless curiosity that made him want to pull the string and unravel the sweater. Nevertheless, he let out a small sigh of relief when she crossed to his table.

"I thought you weren't joining me for a pint?" Kane asked, crossing his arms over his chest. Iris looked good, he thought, refreshed from her flight and casually cool in black leather and her purple boots again.

"I forgot you would be here," Iris answered honestly, causing Kane to throw his head back and laugh. She winced, and then pulled her leather jacket off before taking the chair he slid out for her. "And that makes me sound like a jerk."

"As much as it wounds my soul that I wasn't the first person on your mind after you landed in a foreign country, I'll forgive the insult. Though I do pride myself on being memorable." Kane brought his fingers to his chin, pretending to stroke his nonexistent beard, and pursed his lips.

"Ah yes, very distinguished you are. I can't believe you slipped my mind, even for a moment," Iris said. But his joking worked, and some of the tension lines in her forehead eased as she settled back into her chair and scanned the room. "This is a nice place. Quite the quintessential Irish pub, isn't it? If I was making a movie, this would be the set I'd want to use."

It was an opening for Kane to talk about his work, and he paused for a moment, wondering how much he would share with this woman. His Rock Rebels series was hugely popular, which was why he wrote it under a partial pseudonym. He also realized that if he wanted to learn anything more about Iris, he'd have to be the first to open up. He'd quickly learned that on the drive down to Grace's Cove. While she was a great conversationalist, she was an expert at deflecting personal inquiries. To the point that he wondered if she had to do so a lot in her work, or if it was merely because the ex-boyfriend had really done a number on her.

"Is that right? Tell me what you see," Kane ordered, and Iris's moody eyes danced to his.

"Why?" Iris asked and, again, Kane appreciated her directness.

"I'm a screenwriter." Kane fudged a bit. "I like to learn how other people view the world. You may see something differently than I do."

Interest lit in Iris's face, and she turned once more, taking a more leisurely assessment of the pub.

"Well, in general, I see a well-functioning pub. It's an art, isn't it, to have a place be this busy but not make the clientele feel stressed or unwelcomed. See how it moves? The servers, the bartenders…it's like a dance, really." Iris pursed her lips as she studied the pub, and Kane caught himself staring at her lush lips. "She's the conductor."

Kane pulled his focus away from Iris's face to where a small woman with close-cropped hair and boundless energy pulled a pint while taking an order from a patron. Sliding the pint across the bar, she ducked under the pass-through and stuck her head into the kitchen before turning their way.

"Incoming," Kane said and smiled as the woman breezed to a stop in front of their table.

"Another pint for you?" the woman asked before narrowing her eyes at Iris. She paused for a moment, something flashing in her eyes, and Kane wondered what she saw in Iris. "Welcome to Gallagher's. What's your fancy this evening?"

"I'm under strict orders to tell you to put a pint on Morgan's tab as I'm purchasing a painting," Iris said.

"Well, that's lovely isn't it then? Aislinn does stunning work, she does. I'll be happy to get you a pint. Anything you fancy?"

"Actually, a glass of wine would be nice. A red?"

"I've a lovely cabernet?"

"Perfect," Iris said with a smile. "And a food menu would be great."

"Sure thing." The woman turned and nodded to a passing server, who immediately crossed over and handed them menus. Iris was right. This woman was the conductor. "My name is Cait, and this is my pub. I'm happy to recommend any dishes. Are you two on holiday then?"

"Oh, we're not a..." Iris immediately interjected, looking up from where she paged through the menu.

"We've only just met," Kane said with a smile. "I gave her a lift from the airport. I'll be staying a few months for work, and Iris is visiting."

"That's grand, then. It's always nice to make new friends. If you stay in town long enough, soon everyone will be your friend. We're a tightknit bunch here, and if you want to hear any of the local gossip, this is the spot for it," Cait said. "Now...for food?"

"I'd love some of the potato soup and a side salad," Iris said, and Kane realized he needed to put in an order as well.

"Whatever's on special is fine for me," Kane said, suspecting a Saturday night special would likely be any type of typical Irish fare.

"That's a Shepherd's pie for you, then. Bailey's Irish cream cheesecake for dessert." With that, Cait snagged their menus, disappearing just as quickly as she'd arrived.

"You're right. She's the conductor," Kane agreed.

"But you see how she never made us feel rushed or pressured to order? Efficient and always assessing. Her eyes missed nothing. Did you see how she was constantly scanning?" Iris asked, opening her mouth and then closing it. Kane was certain she had been about to say something else but then stopped herself. A server drifted back with their drinks, and Kane held his up.

"Slàinte," Kane said, and Iris tapped her glass to his before taking a sip. She sighed happily and continued to look around the pub.

"I see families and friends who are well-acquainted with each other. You can tell by the way they sit at their tables or at the bar. See how their chairs are turned out, opening themselves to speaking with others? While those tables"—Iris nodded to several tables across the room— "those are tourists. They're closed off, unsure or not expecting to chat with anyone but their group."

Kane appreciated the way her mind worked. It had been a somewhat joking request, though he was interested in how she viewed the pub, but her analysis was making his brain work in ways that it hadn't in a while.

"As design goes," Iris continued, pursing her lips once more, "it hits the nail on the head for a cozy Irish pub. The dark wood floors, the beautiful wooden bar, the long mirror behind the shelves? It all works. I suspect the mirror is so the bartenders can keep an eye on the crowd while mixing drinks, but the practicality doesn't take away from the appeal. And with all the old-timey Guinness signs and vintage pub advertisements on the wall? Yeah, it works. Plus, I can't resist a fireplace. Nothing beats that for ambience." Iris brought her fingers to her mouth and kissed the tips. And once again, Kane found himself drawn to her lips. She'd be a good kisser, he thought, and then shook his head.

It was the first sexual thought he'd had about a woman

since Alison had left him, and that was certainly something to note.

"I love a good fire as well," Kane said, smiling. "A fire's a gathering point, you know. There's nothing finer than sitting by a fire with a whiskey and sharing stories."

"And you tell them, apparently." Iris turned back to him. Leaning forward, she put her elbows on the table and propped her face in her hands. In the background, someone tuned a fiddle, and Kane's mood picked up. It seemed like they were in for a session.

"I do. In fact, that's what drove me here. I'm to write a screenplay and have a bit of a writer's block going on," Kane said. It wasn't entirely untruthful and about as much as he was willing to reveal at the moment.

"Yes, well, you should be kind to yourself. You're going through a lot. Emotions take time to process, you know," Iris said. "What type of screenplay? Maybe you can murder your ex."

"That's what I suggested to my agent." Kane laughed when Iris winced.

"I really shouldn't be suggesting murder, but leaving you at the altar might warrant it," Iris said.

"Perhaps it warrants a fictional murder. Not a real one, of course." Kane laughed as Cait materialized by their table with a tray.

"No murders on my watch," Cait said smoothly as she deposited food in front of them. "Do I need to be keeping an eye on you two?"

"It's him with the motive." Iris nodded to Kane, neatly throwing him under the bus. "I come in peace."

"And we welcome you," Cait said, and again, something in her tone made Kane think he was missing some-thing. When Cait squeezed Iris's shoulder, and her eyes widened in shock for a moment, he grew even more certain that he was missing an underlying thread.

"Do you know Cait?" Kane asked, forking up some mashed potatoes and blowing on it.

"Nope, this is the first time I've been here. She seems nice, no? Terrifying in her own way, I suppose." Iris took a bite of her salad, drifting into silence for a moment, cocking her head as though she was listening for some-thing. Her brow furrowed, and she shook her head ever so slightly. He wondered what she was talking herself out of. Oh, but this woman was fascinating, Kane decided, and settled in for an interesting night. If he could keep her here long enough.

"I like terrifying women," Kane admitted. "They make for great characters, and they're good people. Tell me, Iris. Do you watch a lot of television? Do you have a favorite show?"

"I'm more of a reader, I'll admit. I'm a diehard romance novel fan, and you can pry them out of my cold dead hands," Iris admitted. Kane's heart lifted, knowing she wouldn't make fun of his genre of choice.

"Any favorites?" Kane asked, pretending nonchalance.

"Mmm, I totally just blew through the Rock Rebels series. I *loved* them. The way she writes…just, yum," Iris sighed, and Kane's breath caught. He could've kicked himself for putting himself in this position. "What's your screenplay about?"

"It's…a romantic comedy, actually," Kane admitted, his cheeks flushing a bit. It was one of the reasons he wrote under a pen name. It wasn't as common for a man to write in the romance genre, so it had been easier for him to write the books of his heart under a pen name.

"Realllllly?" Iris drew the word out. "Color me surprised. I was certain it would be like fantasy death machine war stuff."

"Is that right? Do I strike you as violent?" Kane raised an eyebrow as the fiddler started to play.

"Well, what with all the murdering…" Iris choked on a laugh when Cait, who'd been cruising by their table at that exact moment, shot them both a warning look. "She's going to kick us out soon if we don't behave."

"Music's starting up anyway. It's a good time to be quiet," Kane said, hoping to move past the subject matter of his work. He'd need to come clean with her soon enough if they spent any more time together, but not tonight.

"Do they really just shove into a booth and play like that?" Iris lowered her voice as a thin woman with tangled gray hair started to sing a lively tune.

"Yes, 'tis true. We Irish love a good session. Settle in and enjoy. It's a treat to hear, I'll tell you that much," Kane said, a smile on his lips as he relaxed into the music.

"I have to say…I'm thinking this was a good choice for us both." Iris raised her wineglass to his again. "Instead of nursing broken hearts, we're eating world-class food and listening to beautiful music."

"Is your heart broken, then?" Kane surprised himself by asking, even though he'd just said they didn't have to talk anymore. But he found himself desperately wanting to know the answer.

"It...it *is*. But not for the reasons you'd think," Iris whispered, not wanting to be rude over the music.

"Then why?" Kane pushed the point.

"Because it taught me that I couldn't trust myself. Or others," Iris said, sadness creeping into her eyes as she swayed lightly to the music.

Kane wanted to say something to change her opinion or to give her hope that she wouldn't always feel that way.

But then he'd just be a hypocrite, wouldn't he? Instead, he leaned back in his chair and sipped his pint, wondering how two shattered souls had ended up at the same table together.

CHAPTER 7

"*I* think he's the one," John said late the following morning while Iris lingered over her second cup of coffee and watched the world pass by on the street below.

"You say that with every man you meet," Iris pointed out.

"And I'm not wrong," John said, the sound of the shower running coming through the phone. "Until he's not."

"An optimist at heart." Iris chuckled, crossing her arms and leaning on the window ledge. Her eyes caught on a familiar face, and a warm trickle of…something washed through her as she watched Kane stop and pick up a bunch of mixed flowers on the sidewalk in front of the market across the street.

"More like a romantic. Maybe you'll get there again someday if you can get past Warren," John said. Iris heard the shower curtain rattle on its rungs and knew she'd be put on speakerphone shortly. It wasn't uncommon for them to chat while they got ready for the day, something that had often annoyed Warren. While she'd changed a lot of things for her ex-boyfriend, her friendships were one area that Iris had never capitulated on. The idea of family was somewhat foreign to Iris, as she only had her mother and no siblings or extended family members. The fact she'd managed to procure a small set of loyal friends was something Iris never took for granted.

"I am past him," Iris mumbled absentmindedly, her attention fixated on Kane as he took his time picking out which flowers he wanted. The contrast was appealing to her–this overly handsome and exceedingly masculine man taking his time to examine which delicate bunch of posies he wanted. The fact that he would even think to stop and smell the flowers was also equally appealing.

"Are you really? It's been just over a week since he blew up your world and your business. You're over him already? If that's the case, honey, you never should have been under him," John said, his voice echoing in the bathroom as he showered.

"You're not wrong," Iris said, his words settling inside her. The truth laid down, like the first layer of foundation to build her new life upon, and she felt some of the tension that plagued her begin to ease. "You are absolutely and entirely correct, John. If a man didn't have the ability to shatter me when I left, then what was I even doing with him? I should have seen that a long time ago. I became complacent and accepting because...it was just easier. And this is what the universe has served up. One big heaping lesson with a side of get your shit together on top."

"Life lessons are rarely fun, are they?" John asked. It was something else she appreciated about him. While he certainly enjoyed pointing out when he'd been right about something, John never rubbed people's faces in it. It was as though he wanted his good insights to be noted, a little checkmark next to a line item on a list, and then he'd happily move forward to help however he could. It was one of the many reasons he was the best of friends.

"No, they really aren't." Iris sighed. But it wasn't the sigh of someone sad about a life lesson. She sighed because Kane had turned and laughed at something a passerby had said. She found herself caught on him, his head thrown back and his face alive in laughter, and she committed the image to memory. When his eyes lighted on her, Iris squeaked. "Eeek!"

"What? What's happened? A mouse?" John asked, the shower going off.

Iris ducked from the window, having totally been busted staring, and then took a few breaths to remind herself that she was a grown woman who had every right to look out the window of her apartment, no *flat*, if she wanted. Drawing herself back up, she leaned on the window again to find Kane gone. Her heart fell.

"No, I just got busted staring at a guy..." Iris admitted.

"Oh, tell me more..." John said.

"It was the guy who gave me a ride. Kane. He's buying flowers across the street. We had dinner last night," Iris said and hurried on at John's squeal of delight. "*Accidentally*. We accidentally had dinner last night. He's cool."

"How does one accidentally have dinner after accidentally hitching a ride with him?" John demanded.

"It's a small town, John. It's normal to run into people all the time." She paused as Kane exited the store, a shopping tote on his shoulder with two bunches of flowers in his hand. Looking up, he waved at her, and she grinned, tipping her coffee cup to him. Her eyes widened when he crossed the street to her place, and then she couldn't see him anymore. Was he…? The buzzer sounded in her apartment, startling her so that coffee slopped from the rim of her mug to her hand. "Shit!"

"What? What's happening?" John demanded.

"He just rang my bell. And I spilled coffee on my hand," Iris growled.

"Is he bringing you flowers?" John's voice rose into a squeal, and Iris rolled her eyes. "I am so here for this. Yes, a redemption arc for my Moonie! Get it, girl."

"Nothing to get…except going. Byeeeeeee," Iris trilled into the phone, disconnecting and looking down at her clothes with a sigh. She hadn't been expecting company, so she wore leggings, a simple white T-shirt, and no bra. Her hair was in knots around her head, and she probably had makeup smeared around her eyes. However, she didn't have to impress anyone, did she? It wasn't like she or Kane were interested in dating again anytime soon. They'd both agreed on their mutual distrust for the world. Pressing the button to let him up, Iris quickly scanned the room to see if anything distressing, like her purple silk bra, was lying out, but she'd tidied everything this morning already. That was something she'd learned when she was younger– small spaces didn't lend themselves well to clutter.

"Good morning," Iris called, opening the door and leaning against the doorjamb. She wasn't sure about inviting him into her space, so she waited while he clambered up the steps.

"Good morning…is it still morning?" Kane wrinkled his forehead in question. He looked fresh, a lightness about his face that hadn't been there the last two times she'd seen him. She wondered if Ireland was slowly working its magic on him as it was her.

"It's just past eleven so, yes, still morning." Iris grinned at him. It was hard not to. He was like a burly lumberjack with golden retriever energy. The plaid button-down he wore today added to the outdoorsman feel, and Iris marveled at the woman who had decided to cheat on this man.

"I won't be bothering you, but I figured you might enjoy a few posies as well," Kane said, handing her one of the bunches of flowers he held. Iris's heart caught, and she pursed her lips, surprised at his gesture.

"Really? That's…very sweet of you, Kane," Iris said, a suspicious note in her voice. Kane laughed, reading her clearly.

"Listen, I figured that since I had nobody to buy flowers for anymore, I would buy myself some. And yes, I realize that sounds ridiculous, but I can't keep plants alive for the life of me, so it's nice to have flowers once in a while. And when I saw you in the window, I thought you might appreciate some flowers as well. Because you know what, Iris?"

"What's that, Kane?" Iris said, enjoying his bravado.

"We deserve it." Kane punctuated his words with a finger in the air.

"You're right. We're smart, good-looking, and nice

people. We do deserve flowers." Iris laughed, appreciating the ridiculousness of it all.

"Oh, so she thinks I'm good-looking. Duly noted," Kane said, already on his way back down the stairs. "I'll leave before you skewer me with one of your glares and ruin any false hopes I have."

Iris rolled her eyes even though he did make her smile. He'd been lightly flirting with her since they'd met, and she'd realized last night that was likely just his personality. She wasn't going to read into anything.

"I said *we're* good-looking. It would be rude to compliment myself and not you as well, not when you've brought me flowers and all."

"Oh, a pity compliment. Can I say my ego's crushed enough that I'll lap up any crumbs you throw my way?" Kane called up and, despite herself, Iris laughed.

"Thank you for my flowers."

"Welcome…" Iris just heard the door open, and street sounds filled the stairwell before it shut once more. Amused, she closed the door behind her and dug around until she found an old Mason jar she could put the flowers in. Arranging the bunch, Iris took it over to the windowsill and placed the flowers in the light, and then stepped back. They did look pretty in the apartment. Kane also wasn't wrong. They *did* deserve flowers. Neither of them had done anything wrong in their relationships, so maybe treating themselves on occasion would bolster their moods. Speaking of which…it was time for Iris to go pick up her painting. She'd already cleared a spot for it behind the bed, happy that the singular long shelf that lined the wall would support the painting without her having to nail anything into the wall. She didn't yet know how long she planned to stay, but hanging pictures felt a touch too permanent for her at the moment.

After a shower, Iris pulled on a pair of black jeans, a simple white button-down, and her leather jacket. She left her hair to tumble over her shoulders, hooked in some dangly quartz earrings, and grabbed her crossbody fringed purse. With a last look at the cheerful vase of flowers by the window, Iris left her apartment and made her way outside.

The weather was moody, which suited Iris just fine, and she zipped her jacket as a brisk wind carried over the harbor. The color of the water lent toward slate gray today, with little white caps tipping the waves, and she wondered if they were due for rain. The cold didn't seem to bother any tourists who unloaded from buses and clamored to take pictures of the brightly colored buildings hugging the harbor road. Iris wondered if the bright colors were meant to dispel some of the grayness that came with the gloomy weather. She turned at the gallery just as the first rain drops began to fall and stepped through the door.

Iris noted vanilla and lavender for the candle scent today, appreciating the shop's warmth and coziness. The ceiling held soft track lighting that highlighted the rich colors of the art on the walls, and brightly colored rugs were tossed randomly over the honey-colored wood floors. Today, a different woman stood at the counter, and Iris's eyes caught on her as Ophelia clamored for attention in her brain.

"Talk to her. She's a good one," Ophelia offered, and Iris nodded gently, so Ophelia would know she'd heard. Tuning her out, Iris pasted a smile on her face as the woman turned. Immediately, Iris understood why Ophelia wanted her to engage. She detected the same wisp of otherness about this woman as she had Morgan.

"Hello, welcome. Is there anything I can help you look for today?" the woman asked, clasping her hands in front of her. She wore a knit tunic in rich turquoise and purple with a tumble of crystals at her neck and on her wrists. Her gray hair curled wildly down her back, and her eyes were kind and assessing.

"I've come to pay for the painting I put on reserve yesterday. My name is Iris Dillon," Iris said, and a curious look passed across the woman's face before her smile widened.

"Of course! I'm delighted this painting is going to a good home. Morgan mentioned that you'd connected with it immediately. It surely makes my heart sing to know when my work has found the right owner."

"Ah, you're the artist," Iris said. "I'm in awe of what you've created here. Not only is this a great shop, but your work is stunning. Truly stunning."

"Thank you. It never seems like work when I'm paint-ing, but I'm gratified that people enjoy what I create. I'm Aislinn, by the way. Please, come back with me, and we'll take care of the paperwork," Aislinn said, waving her to the back room where a long table held stacks of photographs and frames. Two armchairs in a soft red plaid pattern were tucked next to a low table, and Aislinn gestured to them. "Have a seat while I grab the folder."

Iris settled in, taking the time to study Aislinn while she sorted through a stack of files on a desk, and wondered what it was about these two women who ran this shop that interested her so. Were they also psychics like her? It wouldn't be totally out of character, not with the crystals and the art, but nothing in the shop really screamed anything mystical. Well, Morgan had mentioned auras, hadn't she? Her eyes trailed to the paintings at the front of the shop, those that were more abstract and done in a myriad of mixed colors.

"Are you on holiday then?" Aislinn asked, drawing Iris's attention from the paintings.

"Something like that. Perhaps an extended stay." Iris laughed. "I suppose I'll call it a sabbatical of sorts."

"Oh, what do you do for work?" Aislinn asked as she returned with a folder and a portable credit card machine. When she handed Iris the folder, Iris opened it to scan the itemized receipt, as well as the paperwork certifying the painting as an original work of art. Included was more information on the artist, and Iris's eyes caught on the word aura again. "Do you actually see auras?"

"I do." Aislinn smiled, settling into the chair next to Iris. She didn't seem deterred by Iris's blunt question nor the fact that Iris hadn't answered her question about work. "It's an ability that drives a lot of my creative work."

"And not all auras are pretty, are they?" Iris asked, thinking of the violent painting she'd first noticed when she'd arrived yesterday.

"No, not all auras are pretty." Aislinn sighed and toyed with a bracelet at her wrist. "While I wish we all could carry a lightness with us, some souls are more troubled than others."

"That's a magnanimous way to put it," Iris said, digging in her purse for her credit card. Turning, she handed it to Aislinn, who squinted her eyes at the little credit card machine as she punched in the numbers.

"It's not in my nature to be absolute about good or evil. Auras change as people grow and learn. Labeling someone in the absolute isn't fair," Aislinn scowled at the machine and then let out a relieved sigh when it began to print out the receipt. "There we go. Sure and this dreadful machine gives me problems more often than not."

"Has that been a challenge for you? Seeing auras? Or having people question your abilities?" Iris found herself asking. Maybe she did feel more than a little lost right now, as normally she wouldn't have asked such an intrusive question. She knew that if someone had asked the same of her, she would have been a bit annoyed.

"It has been, at times in my life, quite a challenge. People don't like to accept things they can't immediately understand. You get labeled as bad or evil, and that's tough to hear, particularly when you want to put good into this world. Luckily, I've found a really strong support system here in Grace's Cove."

"Is that right?" Iris asked, hope blooming inside her.

"Yes." Aislinn met her eyes. "And I think you will too."

"Oh...I..." Iris said, catching on the meaning in Aislinn's look. Bells sounded, signaling the arrival of someone to the shop, and Aislinn stood.

"Be right with you," Aislinn called, poking her head

through the door. Turning back, she walked to a neatly wrapped package on the table. "This is your painting. It's triple wrapped in a waterproof layer, so you'll be fine to carry it home. If it's too large for you to manage, I can have it delivered."

"Oh, right. I think I'll manage. I'm stronger than I look," Iris said, standing.

"I don't doubt your strength." Aislinn measured her with those all-seeing eyes of hers. "But I think you do."

"It's…it's a work in progress," Iris said, her voice soft.

"The painting you purchased?" Aislinn asked, shifting gears so quickly that Iris stumbled to keep up.

"Yes?"

"It's of a cove that's here. Go to it. It may have the answers you seek. It's a nice drive from the village. Don't." Aislinn held up a finger, her voice sharp, and Iris's eyebrows shot up. "And I repeat, *don't* go into the cove. But visit it from the cliffs and see how you feel."

"Um…sure. I'll do that," Iris said, though she thought it was unlikely she would anytime soon. Not until she could rent a car, at least.

"Come see me after you do," Aislinn said and strode forward to hold the shop's front door open so Iris could muscle the painting through it. "It was nice meeting you, Iris. I look forward to getting to know you better."

Her words held a note of finality as though they were already friends, and though it struck Iris as weird, it was also comforting. Her tone brooked no disagreement, and it didn't leave a person wondering whether she'd be welcome in the shop again. Instead, it seemed to suggest that it was only a matter of time before Iris would be back for a cup of tea and a chat about the cove.

And maybe she would be. For now, Iris ducked her head against the soft sheets of rain that misted down from the gray sky and hurried up the street.

She couldn't wait to see her painting on the wall.

CHAPTER 8

*K*ane placed his flowers on the table he'd
dragged from the kitchen to the living
room window that looked out over the harbor. While he'd
originally thought he'd work in the spare bedroom, he
found himself increasingly drawn to the main room with
the beautiful view and the cozy fireplace.

Stories were shared around a fire. And so, Kane found
himself lighting a small fire before he started writing for
the second day in a row and, once more, the words flowed.
Correlation was not causation, he reminded himself, but
noted "build a fire" down as something new to add to his
routine. Who was he to mess with what was actually
working for once?

He found himself picking up the threads of the story
he'd outlined for WorldFlix and weaving them into something else entirely. Well, not entirely, as Grant would have
a literal meltdown if he did that, but enough to shift the
project into something that excited him once more. He was
still writing about the Rebel Prince, rock royalty's favorite

bad-boy son, but he was taking the story in a different direction. Instead of having Rebel Prince meet some illustrious cover model and descend into a high-stakes game of who could out-famous the other, Kane now toyed with putting Rebel Prince in a much more complicated and multilayered situation. He wanted his character not to just win the girl but also to grow in the process. Kane wanted family drama, intrigue, comedy, and an opposites-attract vibe.

At that, his thoughts danced to Iris once more. She wasn't his type. Not that Kane truly had a type, as he had always been grateful when any woman took notice of him but, generally speaking, he'd gone for the buttoned-up girl-next-door type. And just look where that had gotten him, he mused, watching a gull swoop lazily over the water. Iris was...not prim and proper. She swore, wore leather, was thick and shapely in a way that made him want to touch her, and he was certain he'd seen the lines of a tattoo sneaking out from the lifted hem of her shirt. She was complicated. At times bristly and standoffish and, at others, her face came alive with excitement. She was fascinating to watch as she wore her emotions on her face, and Kane found himself wanting to ask for her opinion on his story.

Which was silly, really, since he was a professional writer, and she was...well, she still hadn't actually told him what her work was, had she? Amused that she'd managed to dodge him there, he picked up his phone to text her before he could stop himself. They'd exchanged numbers only after he'd badgered her into taking his, and now he wanted to test the waters.

Why, exactly, he wasn't quite sure. He didn't want a relationship and, if he did, it wouldn't be with a prickly American who wouldn't reveal much about herself. What would that be like for building a foundation of trust? Kane laughed to himself at the thought. And yet, or perhaps *because* of this, it took some of the pressure off their relationship. Their friendship, Kane amended. They'd both sadly acknowledged their inability to trust, not truly, so they were kind of off the hook with each other, weren't they? Which was freeing in its own way. Settled, Kane shot off a text before he could overanalyze anything further.

> Kane: If a man slammed his door in your face and kicked you off his property, but then came to find you and apologized, would you go to dinner with him?

> Iris: Is this some weird role-play fantasy?

Kane chuckled, leaning back in his chair to look at the fire as he thought of a witty response.

> Kane: It sounds like it might be one of yours if that's where your thoughts went first.

> Iris: Is this the adult version of I know you are but what am I?

Kane laughed out loud again, thoroughly enjoying the way her mind worked.

Kane: Answer the question, Iris.

Iris: Fine, um, it would depend on the circumstances. I'd need more details. Did I do something that warranted said slamming of door? Was I being the person I am before I've had coffee who shouldn't be allowed to speak to others? Did I kick his cat? Or am I an innocent, and he's just a grumpy jerk? There are a lot of variables at play here.

Kane: Your job is to protect him from the press. You're basically his handler. He wants to be left alone.

Iris: Hmm, intriguing. But then why would he go after her if he wanted to be alone? She's just doing her job, right?

Kane: Correct. And why should she be willing to have dinner with him after he was mean to her?

Iris: Maybe she's hungry?

Kane laughed again, shaking his head at the phone, delighted with the direction this conversation was going. Thinking for a moment, as her questions were valid, he picked up his phone again.

Kane: I need her to see something in him that makes her want to do more than the basic requirements of her job, which is to protect him from nasty press as he's famous. But he's also being a jerk because he's got some pretty serious wounds and trauma. At this point, he feels the world has turned on him and is acting as such. She'll need to see a spark of...something...that gets her invested in not only protecting him, but in, well, him.

Iris: Even more interesting...I guess it depends on what type of woman your heroine is. If she doesn't take shit from anyone, she'll likely not give this guy a second look. However, if this is her job, and she's determined to win at all costs, she'd still go to dinner. But women are good at compartmentalizing, so she could probably easily do her job while also ignoring what a jerk he is. If you want her to fall for him, she's going to need to see something that appeals to her, and it will depend on what her needs are.

Kane: Explain.

> Iris: Well, does she want to be protected? If so, he needs to save her. Does she want to nurture or protect? Then he needs to show his belly somehow. Expose a wound. Flash a vulnerability. Something that makes her see it's all an act, and he's hurting. Then she can help. Women like to help. I'd go with the second one to start. Unless he can really save her from something at the beginning because women like the hero thing too.

> Kane: Maybe they can save each other.

At that, Kane stared down at his words, his stomach twisting. He shoved back from the table and stood, pacing in front of the fire. Maybe that was the crux of it, as well. Men were always taught to save the girl, but never themselves. Wouldn't it be nice if, for once, the girl saved the guy? It actually sounded kind of nice if he could get past the instinct to prove he was a man who could handle everything. This could be a good route for his character, Kane quickly amended, forcing his thoughts back to his book.

> Kane: That's not a bad shout. Thanks for helping me talk through it.

> Iris: No problem. I accept payment in form of royalty percentages…or, in lieu of such, I'll take a ride if you're up for an excursion one of these days.

> Kane: I don't think WorldFlix will share royalties. I barely got any as it was. A ride it is, milady. Where to?

Iris: There's a cove out of town I'm told is a must-see. I'd like to go have a look.

Kane: Ah, sounds lovely. Will tomorrow work? It's meant to rain all day today.

Iris: Perfect, I can grab snacks from across the street. Oh, the flowers look great. Thanks again.

Kane snapped a picture of himself making a silly face next to his own vase of flowers and was rewarded when she sent a similar picture back. But instead of making a funny face, she just smiled into the camera, tucked into a corner of her sofa, her hair piled loosely on her head. His breath caught as she looked impossibly lovely and warm and…his eyes widened as lust moved low in his gut, and he hardened. That was…well, that was new. He hadn't had any movement down there in a while. Grief would do that to a person, he supposed. Now, as his body responded to Iris's picture, he felt slightly guilty that this woman, who was meant to be a friend only, was giving him these thoughts. Perhaps she was just the catalyst, Kane told himself as he put the phone down and went into the bathroom. He wouldn't pleasure himself to her picture—oh no, that would be rude. But maybe it was just the mere act of having a fun text conversation that had gotten things flowing for him again. Convinced that was the case, Kane stripped and hopped into the shower, enjoying the hot stream of water that beat on his shoulders as he sought a much-needed release. When it was over, Kane stood for a moment, his forehead pressed to the shower wall, gasping for breath.

It was time for him to start living again, he realized. He'd hidden for too long now, and it wasn't good for his mental health. He'd been lying to his friends for months, telling them he was just fine when he clearly hadn't been. But maybe now he could be.

Maybe, if Iris stayed around, they could muddle their way out of messy life situations together. It was easier to commiserate with a friend also stuck in the middle of it, wasn't it? Sometimes, he felt like a storm cloud over his friends' happiness and, more often than not, he defaulted to pretending he was fine.

But he hadn't been fine, had he? His fiancée had cheated on him, and his dog had died.

That, quite frankly, sucked. Maybe it was time he gave himself permission to acknowledge that, no, he wasn't doing all that great.

> Iris: Don't make the woman skinny.

Kane raised an eyebrow at the text he found when he got back to the main room, having pulled on sweatpants and a baggy sweatshirt.

> Kane: Who said I had?

> Iris: Well...okay, I just figured if your character was going to win the famous guy, usually that's like a model or some size zero woman. It would be nice to see more normal bodies on television.

> Kane: There are plus-size models, you know.

Kane smiled at the scowling emojis she sent back to him.

> Iris: I'm aware of the body positivity movement, thank you very much. It's taken some of the pressure off women like me, you know.

> Kane: Women like you? What? Cantankerous?

More scowling emojis.

> Kane: Prickly? Kane inserted a photo of a hedgehog along with the text.

Middle finger emojis were his reward, and he laughed out loud.

Brave? Beautiful? Take my breath away? Kane's finger hovered on the send button, and then he deleted the last two phrases, leaving just the first.

> Iris: Damn you. You have to go and be nice, don't you?

> Kane: I have my moments. Plus, I'm just sweetening you up before I start all that murdering I'm meant to be doing.

> Iris: Right, right. Maybe I should rethink this whole going to an abandoned cove in the middle of nowhere idea.

Kane: Too late. I've already changed my schedule around. I will pick you up at ten in the morning. I'm turning my phone off now. I have to finish my words for the day. It turns out that rainy days are the perfect day to write about skinny models who get rescued by famous men.

Iris: Maybe I'll be the one doing the murdering...

It was silly, really, this banter back and forth, yet it brought a smile to Kane's face and made him excited to go on an excursion with Iris tomorrow. He hadn't been excited about, well, anything in ages. Sitting back down at his laptop, he rubbed his hands together.

It was time to write some romance.

CHAPTER 9

*L*ight-gray clouds blanketed the sky, but no rain fell, and Iris took that as a win. Thus far, her time in Ireland had been spent either getting rained on or hiding from the rain, so to have a day when it was fairly dry was a positive as far as Iris was concerned. She hadn't necessarily planned to take more time with her appearance today, yet when she stood by the mirror that morning getting ready, she'd lingered longer than usual. What did Kane think of her? If he wrote about skinny models and famous people, would he even find someone like her attractive? The thought had been so surprising that she'd found herself rolling her eyes. Iris had reminded herself that she was in no way, shape, or form interested or ready to date and, if so, it certainly wouldn't be with a man who was far too put together and good-looking for someone like her. She needed a man who spilled ketchup from his hot dog down the front of his sweatshirt, not someone who wiped facetiously at his mouth with the corner of his napkin and pulled out chairs and opened doors for her. Perfectionism could be daunting.

When the buzzer sounded at her door, she pulled herself from her thoughts and picked up the tote bag of food she had prepared for their outing. In the end, Iris had braided her hair back from her face, put on a simple green sweater, along with her fitted denim pants and her favorite purple boots. For food, she had gone with easy things to snack on like nuts, fruit, and cheeses, as well as a nice crusty loaf of bread with various little jars of jams that the woman at the supermarket had convinced her to try. It wasn't fancy, but since she didn't really know Kane's tastes, she figured he would be happy with whatever she brought. She had also packed a bottle of wine before remembering the drink driving laws in Ireland and pulled it back out. Now, a little trickle of anticipation rippled through her as she bounded down the steps and out the front door.

Kane waited by his car, holding the door open like the gentleman he was.

"Good morning. It seems the weather is indeed on our side today. And don't you look lovely?" Kane said, immediately coming forward to take the bag off her shoulder and put it in the car's trunk.

Iris smiled her thanks at him and slid into the front seat, buckling the belt around her as Kane rounded the car and got behind the steering wheel. She took a moment to admire how well he seemed to fit into the landscape here. In just the short time since she had been out of her apartment, he'd already nodded at two different people and tugged at the bill of his cap as a cute little old woman had teetered past with her walker. Kane looked particularly

Irish today, she mused. His newsboy cap was distinctly appealing and added an edge to his look. Kane also wore a simple gray heather sweater over a plaid shirt with jeans and rugged boots. Altogether, he looked like he could be a farmer—well, maybe an upscale farmer—about to wander his fields and collect his sheep. But in a much more handsome and rugged way, she supposed.

"So did you murder anyone yesterday?" Iris shot Kane a smile as he pulled away from the curb. He snorted and raised an eyebrow at her.

"It's a romance. You can't be murdering people in a romance, or you won't have anybody left to fall in love with," Kane pointed out. "Don't worry, though. I've saved all my murdering for today."

"Oh good, I was worried that today would be boring. I'll be sure to stay on my toes," Iris said. She relaxed back into her seat, drinking in her surroundings as Kane directed the car along a winding road that took them from the village. Iris had spent much of the day before poring over some of her business documents, speaking with the police, as well as looking through her to-be-read list. It was fascinating, really, that she wasn't capable of filling her down time. Now that her business had essentially ground to a stop, Iris just didn't know what to do with herself. That had to be why she'd been overly excited about their excursion today. It would get her out of her apartment and give her an opportunity to explore somewhere new.

Even unwrapping and setting her painting up hadn't taken all that much time, though Iris had enjoyed the thrill that trickled through every time she looked at her very own piece of art. Something was so romantic and magical about the scene in the painting that, time and time again, Iris had found herself staring at it, her mind wandering. There clearly was a community of people here who had some extra-sensory abilities and, despite her recent difficulties, Iris was intrigued. Would they have heard of her? Would they accept her into their community even if they thought she might be a fraud? Or was it time for Iris to take a new path in her life?

Those thoughts had kept her up much of the night, and it had taken three cups of coffee this morning before Iris had started to feel like a functioning human.

"So what do we know about this cove?" Kane asked. "And why are we heading to this particular cove? I'm sure there are loads of them along the coastline. Is this the cove that Grace's Cove is named for?"

"We're going to this cove because I bought my first piece of real artwork yesterday, and it is a depiction of this aforementioned cove," Iris said, a happy note in her tone. "And the artist herself suggested that since I loved the painting so much, I should go see the cove in person." Well, Aislinn had said more than that, but Iris wasn't ready to freak Kane out quite yet. Though she thought they were closer to discussing more about their personal lives and, depending on how she felt about today, maybe she would just open up to him about what she was dealing with. She would play that by ear.

"Well, I'm always up for a good cove exploration," Kane said as he slowed the car for a narrow turn. "I used to spend many hours as a kid clamoring over rocks and trying to find different critters in rock pools along the coast."

"Unfortunately, I have been warned not to go into the

cove," Iris said sheepishly. "In fact, more than one person has now mentioned it to me. I don't know if it's local superstition or if there's actually danger to be found there, but we're not supposed to go into the cove."

"So we're just going to go look at it?" Kane asked with a soft chuckle.

"I guess? On the bright side, if it doesn't start raining, we'll have a nice lunch with a pretty view," Iris said optimistically.

"So really you've invited me along not to go *to* a cove, but to go *look* at a cove. That would be like me inviting you for a drink, but just to look at a bottle of wine and not actually imbibe in one," Kane teased.

"Hey, it's not me with the weird rules. It's this town. I figure we better follow them as we're the newcomers here," Iris grumbled as Kane slowed and let another car inch past on the narrow road.

"Fair enough. I feel like I do remember something about a dangerous cove now that I think about it. It was something to do with the riptides or swimming at the beach. I can't really remember, but I do recall the locals being very pushy about us not venturing to the cove the last time I was here. In fact, that actually makes me wonder why they suggested that you go this time," Kane asked.

"Maybe they realized I would follow directions and not put myself in danger?" Iris arched an eyebrow at Kane.

"Touché, pretty lady, touché. Knowing me, I probably would've scrambled into the cove and gotten myself in some sort of trouble that would have made me the laughing stock of the town." Kane smiled. Iris decidedly ignored how her body warmed when he referred to her as pretty. It was just a casual phrase, she reminded herself.

A song came on the radio that had Kane's lips curving up, and he reached over to turn the dial.

"Do you know this band? The Pogues? I swear this was the music of my childhood. It was always on in the background."

"*Of course.* They get played quite often in Southie, in Boston. It's a fairly Irish part of town." Iris smiled and lapsed into silence. Shane MacGowan's voice filled the car, achingly beautiful in a scratchy and irreverent way, and any lingering tension from dealing with issues with her ex-boyfriend yesterday slid from Iris. The road they followed was a bit precarious, with steep cliffs that shot down to the ocean on the left side and a ragged rock wall on the right. At times, there was only enough room for one car and, more than once, Kane had to pull his car to the side in order to let a stream of vehicles pass by. It kind of felt like they were hanging on the edge of the world, and Iris found herself humming along to the music. Her eyes caught on where the ocean kissed the horizon and, for a moment, Iris could forget her troubles. Maybe that was the entire point of travel. She got to leave everything behind her and live in the moment.

It wasn't long before Iris saw a little stone cottage and pointed at a dirt road to the left of it.

"You're supposed to follow this road, I'm told."

"Your wish is my command," Kane said. Turning the car from the main road, they bumped along the dirt lane until they reached a low stone wall that prevented them from proceeding farther. Kane pulled the car to a stop.

"Do you want me to grab your tote bag from the trunk? Or do you want to explore a little bit first?"

"I'll just bring the tote with me. It's not all that heavy," Iris said. But, of course, Kane got the tote from the trunk and put it on his shoulder instead of handing it to her. They walked in companionable silence across the green field and along a narrow dirt path that led to the cliff's edge. There, a little wooden door stood as a gate to a trail leading farther down the cliff. Someone had placed a picnic table next to it, and Kane dropped the tote bag onto the table before proceeding to the cliff's edge. Iris walked to him and then stopped, her heartbeat picking up speed as she stared at one of the most beautiful natural landscapes she had ever seen. They were high up, higher than Iris had even anticipated, and the steep drop down to the water dizzied her for a moment. Steadying herself, she took a few deep breaths and opened her senses.

Love. That was the first thought that filled her. There was a lot of love in this cove, and the magnitude of it washed over her. Iris understood why people wanted to protect this space. There was very clearly magic here, and not just the kind found in the beauty of nature. Though it *was* beautiful, starkly and devastatingly so. The cliff walls hugged the ocean in an almost perfect C, the sheer walls dropping directly down into the moody blue water that lapped gently onto a golden sand beach far below them. She could see now why her painting had been titled *The Beginning*. Because in a place like this, it was easy to believe that all new beginnings could stem from these waters.

"Okay, I retract my earlier statements about it being

silly to just go look at a cove and not go into said cove." Kane rocked back on his heels, his hands in his pockets. "This is breathtaking, yet a part of me does feel it would be unsafe to try to navigate that narrow path all the way down to the water. Perhaps they've had one or two tourists take a tumble and hurt themselves. And I can't blame them for not wanting that to happen again. We are a fair ways away from any sort of medical help at the moment."

"I'm absolutely fine with just enjoying the cove from up here for now," Iris said. "Shall we have a seat and soak in all this beauty? At least while the rain holds off?" Iris eyed the clouds suspiciously, seeing they had darkened since leaving the village.

"I think that would be the prudent choice," Kane said, a note of relief in his voice.

They turned, but not before Iris caught a flash of turquoise-blue light shining from the depths of the water. She paused, her heart hammering in her chest as the light pulsed with the flow of the waves before winking from sight. Had she imagined that moment? Or was it a trick of the sunlight? She peered once more at the darkening clouds, but no wayward streams of sunlight had broken through.

"Pay attention," Lara whispered in her head. Iris was immediately annoyed. To what? The glowing water? To Kane? To her feet so she didn't trip and tumble over the edge of the cliff? Grumbling at her spirit guides, she joined Kane at the table where he unpacked the food she'd brought.

"So what did you do with your day yesterday while I was playing in my made-up world?" Kane asked, and Iris studied him for a moment. She realized she wanted to tell him what she was dealing with because his opinion now mattered to her for some reason. Why it mattered to her was a thought for another time, and Iris tucked that away. However, when she asked her spirit guides again if Kane was trustworthy, they assured her he was. Which meant if she wanted to take the leap into truly making a friend here, Kane was a worthy candidate. He also seemed genuinely interested in her life.

"Do you really want to know?"

"Well, when you say it like that ... I'm not sure." Kane gave her a worried look.

"That's fair. It did sound a bit daunting, didn't it?" Iris laughed. "I was actually working with the police for much of the day as they are trying to track down my ex-boyfriend and see if he has stolen from anyone else on top of having stolen from me."

"I'm so sorry you have to deal with this. Is there anything I can help with?" Kane asked, his handsome face creased with worry. "Do they have any leads?"

"No, no leads. Frankly, on the scale of major crimes that the Boston Police force must deal with, well, this one is not as serious. However, it's serious to me." Iris shrugged and took a cube of cheese to nibble on. Her eyes tracked back out to where the water crashed against the cliff walls, and she took strength from the cove.

"Well, of course it's serious to you. He stole your money." Kane's hands closed in a fist as though he would punch Warren if he could.

"It's more than that. It's not just the money." Iris looked back at Kane and steadied herself before blurting out her truth. "He's also destroyed my business and ruined my reputation. You see, I'm a psychic medium and...a quite famous one at that. Warren sold a pack of lies to a tabloid, which has now gotten picked up by a ton of other magazines, proclaiming that I'm a fraud. Which isn't true, of course. But when you spend a lifetime battling skeptics, it doesn't take much to destroy the reputation you've built for yourself. Now I'm alone, standing in the mess of what he's left behind. All my clients have canceled, and my reputation is in ruins. And so I guess the money he stole from me doesn't seem as important as what he's actually done to my life." Iris watched Kane carefully, wondering how he would take the news.

"Wow. Okay, so there's a lot to unravel here. First of all, can I just say how cool is that?" Kane's eyes lit with excitement, and Iris tilted her head at him.

"You think it's cool that my ex-boyfriend ruined my business and my reputation?" Iris shook her head as she clucked her tongue sadly. "You really are a twisted man, aren't you?"

"No! I mean, I won't argue that I'm twisted. I just meant that being a psychic sounds really fascinating, and I'm probably going to ask you a billion questions about that after we figure out how to find and murder Warren." At that, Iris felt a laugh bubbling up inside her. Perhaps sharing her truth wouldn't be so bad after all.

"Here we are, back to the murder again. Maybe Cait is right to want to keep an eye on us," Iris teased.

"But in all seriousness, I'm really sorry for you, Iris. Not only do you have to deal with someone violating your trust but they've also hurt your livelihood. It makes total sense to me why a trustworthy reputation in your field would matter. It must have taken you years to build up your business. I mean…I guess I also understand *why* there are skeptics. Unfortunately, it does seem to be an area that grifters are drawn to."

"It's true, unfortunately. Because most of my clients… when they come to me? They're often at a particularly vulnerable point in their life. Which means they may not be thinking clearly. Or they're looking for hope and answers. A lot of frauds out there profit on giving people hope or, you know, leading them down a path of having to arrange for more appointments before they're healed or have them pay to remove a supposed curse…that kind of thing," Iris said with an angry shake of her head. "It's really frustrating to me because I want my clients to succeed unless of course I sense that they're horrible people, and then I don't, but that's usually few and far between. Otherwise, I truly want the best for the people who come to me, and I want to be able to guide and help them in any way that I can. Now, well, I don't know if I'll ever be able to work in this industry again." Iris's breath caught as she looked back out at the water.

The truth of it was, Iris loved what she did for a living. She didn't want to have to stop doing it. But right now? She didn't know how to see her way out of the mess Warren had created for her. It hurt, knowing that she might not be able to move forward in the way she wanted.

"Well, I can't say I know a lot about your industry. However, I do know a lot about something else," Kane said, surprising her by reaching across the picnic table and taking one of her hands. Once again, that jolt of electricity raced up her palm, and she closed her eyes for a moment, reveling in the warmth of his touch.

"What's that?" Iris asked, keeping her tone light.

"I'm *really* good at research, and I'm *really* good at solving other people's problems." Kane laughed. "A part of being a writer is throwing my characters into a bunch of problems and then figuring out how to get them out of it. So if you'll allow me, I'd like to be able to help you."

"Aren't you supposed to be helping yourself?" Iris asked, arching a brow at Kane. "If I recall, you are also going through an equally devastating time, aren't you?"

"Well, maybe we can help each other, then," Kane amended. He smiled at her, hope in his eyes, and Iris found that she didn't have it in her to say no to him. In fact, she found that she very much wanted to say yes to him in more ways than one. When *that* thought entered her mind, she quickly disengaged her hand from his, not wanting to lead the conversation in the wrong direction. She would take his offer as friendship and nothing more.

"Okay, Kane. It looks like we've become each other's projects, haven't we?" Iris said and then jumped when a bark startled her. Turning, she looked over her shoulder as a dog raced across the field to them, her ears streaming behind her in the wind.

"See?" Kane asked, excitement in his voice. "A dog appeared when we decided to help each other. There is no stronger blessing."

A woman followed the dog, her feet shoved into Wellies, and a loose sweater pulled over her curvy frame. Strawberry-blond hair tumbled down her back, and she regarded them with warm whiskey-brown eyes.

"Rosie told me people were down here, but I didn't realize who it was." At her words, Iris immediately stiffened. This was it. The moment that she had been nervous about. She had finally been recognized from all of the magazine articles that had been written about her. Closing her eyes, she took a deep breath and steadied herself before pasting a smile on her face.

"And who do you think is down here?" Iris found herself asking with just a note of bitchiness in her voice.

"Well, you're kin of sort to me." At her words, shock filled Iris, but there was no time to process, as the sky took that moment to open up and drop sheets of rain on their heads.

CHAPTER 10

"Thanks," Kane said, accepting the towel that Gracie, the woman who had appeared at their picnic table, offered him. They stood just inside the front door of the stone cottage they'd passed on their way to the cove, stamping their feet and patting the rain from their faces.

For a moment, when Gracie had said she knew who they were, he'd worried that she was about to spill his author's name to Iris. Not that it should matter all that much. She'd just told him she was a psychic, hadn't she? Didn't that mean she probably already knew all his secrets? Or was that mind-reading? Or could they do both? Now, his brain scrambled as he tried to recalibrate his thoughts about the woman he'd become somewhat entranced with.

Interesting choice of words, Kane lectured himself, as he took in the long line of shelves that hugged one wall of the cottage, cluttered with hundreds of tiny bottles with neat labels. A large wooden table dominated the space, and it looked to serve as both a workspace and a place for meals based on the line of small bottles and jars that stood empty next to a bowl that Gracie picked up. She sniffed it and then reaching for a small jar, added a dash of herbs and stirred the mixture. Kane couldn't be sure if it was food or creams but based on the scent of roses wafting his way, he figured she must be making some sort of facial cream.

The cottage was cozy in the way of spaces that had long been lived in, and every corner was used economically. Kane turned to see a small sitting area jutting off to the right, which held a carved wooden rocking chair, a small fireplace, and another oversized armchair. A large dog bed sat on the floor next to the fire, and Rosie, the dog, padded over and curled up with a contented sigh. A small kitchenette, with a sink located directly beneath a wide window looking out to the sea and framed by cheerful red poppy curtains, was situated to his left. Kane felt instantly at home, for he'd grown up running in and out of many similar cottages as these, and he wondered if Gracie had grown up here.

"I'll just be taking those from you." Gracie held out her hand for their towels and then disappeared through one of two doors at the other end of the cottage. A low murmur of voices sounded, and Kane realized she wasn't alone here.

"Are you okay?" Kane asked, turning to look down at Iris, whose eyes had followed Gracie's movements. He had to imagine that discovering relatives, and ones that apparently knew you, was a bit disconcerting.

"Jury's out on that," Iris muttered. Pursing her lips, she

tilted her head, nodding a few times like she had the other night, and it dawned on Kane what she was doing. What he had thought was an odd quirk of hers, like tugging on an earlobe when stressed, was instead her likely tuning into her second sight. He had *so* many questions. Now was probably not the time, Kane thought, and instead watched Iris conduct some sort of internal debate with herself. When her eyes cleared, refocusing and realizing he was staring at her, she shrugged and gave him a lopsided grin.

"Occupational hazard," Iris said. She tapped her forehead with one finger. She seemed lighter now that she could speak openly about herself, and Kane found he was even more interested in getting to know this fascinating woman. "I was checking in with my spirit guides."

"You can hear them?" Kane asked. He kept his voice low, not wanting to reveal anything to Gracie that Iris wasn't comfortable with sharing.

"Yes, they speak directly to me. It took me a long time to figure out what was going on and, let me tell you, it was a relief to realize what was actually happening. For a while, I thought I was becoming detached from reality."

"I suppose that would be jarring," Kane murmured. He paused, his hands in his pockets, and rocked back on his heels as he thought about what that must have been like for Iris. It must have been strange to have voices speaking to her, independent of her own thoughts, and if that was how her powers manifested for her then, surely, she must have questioned her sanity a time or two. He would have, that was for certain. But at the same time, it spoke of her confidence as a person that instead of dismissing these voices, she had explored what that meant for her. It took a certain level of courage to muscle through an experience like that and then develop those skills into a successful business. Layers, Kane thought to himself. She had so many layers to her.

"I'm sorry to keep you waiting. I had to interrupt King of the World himself to end a business call and extract himself from buying another country or whatever he was doing." Gracie sniffed and then laughed when a man dressed in pressed slacks, a white button-down, and a striped tie stepped from the room behind her and poked her in the ribs. He carried himself as someone comfortable negotiating million-dollar deals in high-level boardrooms and looked decidedly out of place in this homey Irish cottage.

And yet the ease of which he moved around the room spoke of his comfort here. Interesting, the juxtaposition of the two. Kane was already making character notes in his mind as the couple stopped in front of them.

"Iris, I'd like to formally introduce you to Dylan Kelly, your great-great-great...hmmm I'm not sure how many greats, actually. Grandfather, though is where I'm getting at."

Kane's mouth dropped open, and his eyes flew to Iris's face. Was she buying this nonsense? Surely, Gracie had simply misspoken, and she meant that Dylan was descended from Iris's father?

"Wait." Gracie turned and pinched her nose, looking up at Dylan, who wore an amused smile on his face. "You wouldn't be her grandfather if you were her father, right? So what does that make you?"

"I wasn't *her* father. And in this life? A descendent is

all." Dylan wore an easy smile as he came forward, his hand outstretched to Iris. "My apologies for the convoluted nature of things. It's…tricky to explain."

"It doesn't have to be tricky if you're just honest about it." Gracie shrugged.

"Not everyone handles the mystical with the same ease you do, my love," Dylan said, shaking Iris's hand. Turning, he offered his hand to Kane.

"I'm Kane." Kane only offered his first name and accepted Dylan's firm shake and coolly assessing look.

"Nice to meet you both. Can I put on a cup of tea for you? I think we have some catching up to do," Dylan asked.

"Yes, please," Iris said. She pursed her lips together, her head tilted at that angle again, and Kane watched Gracie watching Iris. Gracie's eyes narrowed and then widened, and Kane wondered if she'd picked up on Iris's abilities.

Fascinating lot, these people were. Ideas for stories were already swirling in his mind, and he had to tamp down his enthusiasm that yelled at him to pull a notepad from his pocket to start cataloging details.

"Please, sit," Gracie said, turning to clear the bottles. Iris and Kane sat next to each other on the long bench on one side of the table while Dylan brought cups and a teapot over. "Sorry for the mess. I was in the middle of making a new arthritis cream."

"Ah, you're a chemist, then?" Kane asked since Iris continued to be silent, her wide eyes tracking Dylan.

"Nope, I'm a healer. Among other talents," Gracie said, a smile hovering on her lips as she watched Iris's reaction closely. Iris raised her eyebrows but, still, she said nothing.

"There we go, that'll be set to steep for a moment," Dylan said as he brought a packet of biscuits to the table. "Now, let's explain ourselves a little more clearly before Iris runs for the hills."

"I'm not..." Iris stopped and shook her head. "I'm listening."

"Do you believe in reincarnation, Iris?" Gracie asked, taking a biscuit from the pack and nibbling on the corner.

Kane's mouth dropped open. He couldn't help it. This was not where he was expecting the conversation to go. Instead, he'd thought that maybe Gracie would haul out an old book with a weathered family tree on the pages.

"Of course I do," Iris said. She twisted a purple crystal that hung on a chain around her neck. "Is that what you're getting at? Dylan's a reincarnation of family in my past life?"

Kane's eyes flew to Dylan, the one who looked the least likely to accept any of this and instead found the man to be at ease with the conversation. Interesting, Kane noted.

"Not the entire family, just one man," Dylan clarified. "It seems that I was the father of your great-great...well, however many generations it would be, grandmother."

"How do you spell your name?" Iris asked, continuing to twist the chain around her finger.

"In the now? Dylan. But, in that life, my name was spelled Dillon." Dylan took the time to spell out the name, and Iris's eyes widened.

"Dillon is my last name. Iris Moon Dillon."

"*You're* Iris Moon?" Gracie gasped, putting her hand to her lips.

"Yes," Iris said, her face freezing when she suddenly realized what she'd revealed.

"I had no idea you had another name. Oh, this makes so much sense now," Gracie crowed. She did a little dance in her chair, shaking her head back and forth. "I've admired your work, you know. Phenomenal career you've had. And *of course* you've got power. Everybody touched by me does."

"I'm sorry…what?" Iris said, blinking rapidly at the still dancing Gracie, and Kane was with her on this one. It was just too much to process quickly.

"Gracie, as you see her today, is the reincarnated soul of Grace O'Malley," Dylan explained. "When she and I met in another lifetime, we fell deeply in love, but our time together was brief. When I was murdered, Grace avenged my death but never stopped loving me. Later, upon her own death, Grace walked into the cove you see there, and her powerful magic enchanted her bloodline for generations to come. Sacrifice in death, you see? That same night, as Grace died, her daughter gave birth on the same beach. More powerful magick. However, what we've recently learned, cheeky wench that she is, Grace loved so strongly that she also afforded magickal protection and powers to those of the man she loved. My bloodline."

Kane was kicking himself for not having a recorder for all this information. He turned to Iris, who sat frozen. Putting an arm loosely around her shoulders because it seemed she needed time to process, Kane raised an eyebrow at Dylan.

"That's...okay, so that's a lot to wrap our heads around, isn't it? But I guess the gist of what you're saying is that Grace, in that time, was able to protect the bloodline of her own and those she loved. Is Iris Grace's family, then?"

"No." Dylan winced. "It appears I had a child at home that I hadn't met yet. I was a sailor, you see, and out to sea to help with the battles."

"Ah, I'm sorry?" Kane wasn't sure if an apology was appropriate for something that had likely happened centuries before.

"Thank you. Iris, we've only just learned about your branch of the family, and I've been looking into finding and contacting you. You...well, you have more family you likely don't know about," Dylan said, his tone kind, and Kane felt Iris stiffen beneath his arm.

"I have more family? I have family?" Iris's voice squeaked.

"You do. If you're willing to accept them, of course," Dylan hurried on, seeming to sense Iris's tension. "It's probably a lot to take in, so whatever you're comfortable with, really."

"I don't know how to be comfortable with a family. I've only ever had my mother. What does that even mean, family? Like sisters and brothers? Cousins? Do I show up for holidays now?" Iris asked. Kane felt a slight tremble move over her and understood just how deeply this must be hitting her.

"No, Iris. We have no expectations of you. Other than to hopefully get to know you a bit, if you'll allow us to. You're welcome here, in our home," Dylan said.

"And, unlike Dylan, who is much more respectful and kind than I am, I'll likely arrive on your doorstep, force you to stay in Grace's Cove, and pepper you with a thousand questions. My love is more of the aggressive sort, so you're kind of stuck with me now," Gracie said, finishing her biscuit.

"But…we're not related." Iris narrowed her eyes at Gracie.

"Sure, we are. This one's my husband. That means you're family. Plus, I gave you powers, didn't I? Ungrateful one, isn't she. Kids these days." Gracie clucked her tongue though she couldn't hardly be much older than Iris.

"My wife can be a touch abrasive." Dylan held up a hand as Gracie rounded on him. "But we love her, nonetheless. I think she is trying to say, in her own way, that we'd like to get to know you further if you're comfortable with that."

"I…I don't know. I *think* that I am?" Iris looked at Kane as though he could answer this for her, and he just shrugged.

"It's whatever you're comfortable with, Iris. It doesn't sound like they are forcing family down your throat. Well, maybe Gracie is, but you can probably just sit with this a moment and see how you feel. Can you tell us any more about the family? The ones related to Iris, that is?" Kane asked, squeezing Iris gently. She remained at his side, leaning into him, and Kane realized how much he enjoyed her warmth. She fit well.

"We're still tracing the bloodline, to be honest," Gracie said. She drummed her fingers on the table and plopped her chin into her hand. "We've met your cousin, which is how we just learned about you. From there, we've tracked a few aunts and uncles. I'm guessing that your grandmother went on to marry and have children, so it's hard to say how much of my magick was imbedded in those that came next. I don't think I was thinking all that much when I was working the enchantment, what with facing my impending death and knowing that I was stepping over into the veil for a while. It's...an unsettling feeling, I'll admit."

"I can imagine," Iris murmured.

"Your cousin is here. Well, not here, here. He's in Dublin right now, likely at practice. You may have heard of him. Mac? William MacGregor? He plays rugby."

"No way!" Kane exclaimed. He was a huge rugby fan, so the fact Iris was related to someone famous excited him. Maybe he'd get to go to a match with her.

"You've heard of him?" Iris looked up at him, forehead creased in concern.

"*Of course*, I've heard of him. Most of Ireland has heard of him. He's, like, a media darling. It's going to be so much fun for you to meet him," Kane said.

"He's famous. Which means paparazzi," Iris said, hunching her shoulders, and Kane realized then why this might upset her.

"Or maybe we wait on that introduction..." Kane turned to Gracie. "Iris is dealing with a lot right now. I'm not sure she'll want to be adding any more fodder to any headlines."

"Oh..." Dylan's eyebrows rose. "Right. I get what Gracie was saying now. Yes, I have heard of you recently.

You're the psychic in the States that everyone is calling a fraud, now, aren't you?"

"Bollocks," Gracie griped. "Such shite, really. This always happens when people refuse to believe what's in front of their eyes. Of course you have powers, don't you? I gave them to you. You're a natural. Don't fuss too much over those stories, Iris. You can start over here. We'll all support you."

"I…what?" Iris blinked at Gracie, a dazed expression on her face.

"Well, why wouldn't ye? You've got family here. Friends. And we all have our own special abilities, so we're used to defending our own. Surely you still want to work, don't you? You're too young to walk away from it all, right?"

"Um…I haven't thought that far…" Iris trailed off with a stunned look on her face. "I'm still reeling from it all."

"Her ex-boyfriend sold a story to the papers. And he stole from her. She's been betrayed and had her name plastered across all the blogs. All her appointments have been canceled. I think she probably needs a moment to breathe before making any decisions on what to do next, right?" Kane spoke for Iris as she sat there with her mouth gaping open.

"What's the ex-boyfriend's name?" Dylan was already typing into a sleek little laptop he'd opened.

"Warren…" Iris said, and then gave Dylan all of his contact information and the little she knew about his betrayal. "The police should be working on it, but we'll see."

"I'll have a look into it as well, if you don't mind me

nudging around a bit?" Dylan's eyes gleamed, and Kane's estimation of the man grew.

"Oh, let him play, Iris. He'll probably break into Warren's accounts and have the man living on the street by the end of the day. He loves this stuff."

"Sure, I guess. I mean…that wouldn't be really nice, would it?" Iris said, and Gracie glared at her.

"Was it nice when he singlehandedly destroyed your reputation? Do you know how long it takes to build trust in the public? No, we're not here to do nice, Iris. We're here to make things right."

"I like her," Kane said to Iris, not muffling his voice, and Iris grinned.

"So do I. I think I'll keep her," Iris said.

"I knew I'd wear you down. Now, let's get down to brass tacks." Gracie rubbed her hands together and bent her head with a look of glee on her face.

CHAPTER 11

The rain hammering the windshield matched Iris's tumultuous thoughts as Kane slowly drove them home, taking his time on the slick road. As they drew nearer to the village, Iris's nerves kicked up. She wasn't sure if she could bring herself to sit at home alone with her thoughts tonight and, at the same time, she didn't think she was in the right mental state to sit alone at a pub either. It was weird, having so much time on her hands, and adding in all of these new factors in her life made it almost impossible to ignore all the emotions churning in her gut.

Before she could open her mouth to ask Kane what he was doing that evening, he turned down a different road and drove the car around the edge of the village.

"Where are we going?" Iris asked, spinning to look at his profile in the fading light.

"I'm abducting you," Kane said, then shot her a smile when he caught her surprised look. "With your permission, of course."

"Is that right? A hostile takeover of my evening plans?" Iris asked, warmth blooming inside her.

"Something like that. I'm getting the vibe that today was a lot for you and, if you're anything like me, you'll probably just go back to your apartment and mope about it. Or whatever your mood may be after processing this new information. My thought is...why don't we go to my place, order a pizza, and watch something funny on the television?"

"You want to WorldFlix and chill?" Iris raised an eyebrow at him.

"I want to hang out with you in a less stressful environment than a pub while enjoying a greasy pizza and laughing at some mindless entertainment. If that's not to your taste tonight, no problem," Kane clarified.

"Actually, that sounds perfect. I'll admit, I was going to ask you what your plans were tonight. My apartment doesn't even *have* a television. Though I guess I could stream a movie on my laptop. Honestly, I don't even know? It's been so long since I've had free time. The thought alone terrifies me. It's just so much...*thinking* time," Iris admitted.

"While it's likely good that you spend some time processing these new developments, as well as just the shit show of your breakup, I don't know that it's required that you do so twenty-four seven. How about you take the night off and just be you for a bit? I'll be your wingman in avoiding all things emotional, and our therapists can shake their heads in disapproval somewhere." Kane pulled the car to a stop in front of a charming stone cottage situated on the hill behind Grace's Cove. He turned, a question on his face. "Thoughts? Feedback? Input?"

"I don't have a therapist," Iris said with a small smile. "I don't know whether the profession would be receptive to my abilities. The minute I walk into an office and start talking about the voices in my head, well, probably things won't go so good for me."

"That's a fair point." Kane tapped his fingers on the steering wheel. "I stopped seeing my therapist a while ago. Kept wanting me to heal my inner child."

"That didn't go well for you?" Iris asked, opening her door. She was more than up for an evening of pizza and movies. While so far, Kane had lightly flirted with her, she didn't feel any trepidation about spending time alone with him in his place. He'd been kind to her today, taking her news and Gracie's bombshell in stride. She didn't see him as being the type to pressure her into a situation that she wasn't comfortable with, and her spirit guides had promised her that he was trustworthy. Tonight really could just be pizza and movies between friends, with no other expectations placed upon it.

"It appears my inner child is an asshole," Kane said as he unlocked the door and stepped inside, flicking the light switch. He moved across the room to a table, gathering his laptop and a pile of papers, and gestured with his full arms. "I'm just going to put this in the other room, and then we can call for food."

"No rush," Iris said, walking to the windows that lined the front room. Night had drawn close, but the rain continued to spatter against the glass, making the lights of the village blur out like a moody watercolor painting.

Energy buzzed through her, and Iris felt like she wanted to dance out of her skin. She began to pace, as was her habit when something was on her mind, and looked up at Kane's laugh.

"Pacing already? Wine may help this situation."

"You're likely not wrong," Iris admitted, following him into the kitchen, where he pulled out a bottle of red and held it up for her approval. Iris squinted at the label and then shrugged one shoulder. "I'm not fancy, and I don't really know enough about wines to pretend to be."

"But you do like wine?" Kane asked.

"I do. I just never took enough time to learn much about it. I'm not a heavy drinker. It...can cloud things for me." Iris tapped a finger to her head as she leaned against a counter and watched Kane uncork the bottle. Interest lit his face, and Iris prepared herself for the incoming questions. She was used to them, as people usually hammered her with questions as soon as they learned about her profession. That or they walked away. It typically depended on their beliefs.

"Interesting. I didn't think about that but, yes, I suppose alcohol would dull things for you, no? That's probably not ideal for work," Kane said. "I'll admit, I'm a curious sort, which means I have a ton of questions. But I don't want to bother you, so will you let me know if I step over the line? Or if you're not in the mood for questions?"

Iris realized it was nice to be asked first. Rarely did anyone ask her if she was in the right frame of mind to have what, in reality, were highly personal discussions about how her abilities worked.

"Hit me with 'em, Kane. I can take it." Iris smiled and

tapped her glass to his before following him back out to the living room. There, she curled up on one end of the deep couch and watched as he bent to the fireplace. His shirt tightened across his back, and Iris raised an eyebrow at the muscles that rippled there. Kane might be a writer, but he certainly spent some of his time away from his desk to get muscles like that.

"How do you balance the two? Like...for example, having a conversation with me but also potentially having a conversation with someone else? Is it a tricky thing to navigate them?" Kane asked, striking a match against the stone mantel.

"It was, at first, because I've had this essentially my whole life. As a child, I thought they were imaginary friends. As I grew older, I realized that other people didn't have the same internal dialogue as I did. Now, *that* was a steep learning curve." Iris laughed and took another sip of her wine, pulling a soft throw blanket over her lap. "Here I'd be at school asking kids about things in their life like it was common knowledge. Trust me, that didn't go over well when parents were divorcing or new siblings were on the way...anything like that. However, once I fully came to understand what I was working with, *then* I was able to learn how to mute my guides."

"Mute them?" Kane brushed his hands off on his legs and stood, bringing his wine with him as he crossed the room and took a seat on the other end of the couch from her. "Sure and that's an interesting way to put it. Then you're saying you don't have to, like...I don't know...do a ritual or something to bring them to you? I've seen something like that on a show, I think. Where the psychic starts with a little prayer or something and then brings the spirits in. Is that not the case for you then?"

"It depends on what I'm trying to accomplish." Iris realized she enjoyed talking about her process with someone genuinely interested in her work. "On a day-to-day basis, my personal spirit guides are with me. I can unmute them and communicate as needed, whenever and wherever. I don't need to speak to do so. I can just communicate with my thoughts. However, in a reading with a client, I'm quite often not speaking with my guides but theirs. That requires a little more finesse, as I need to tune in to their guides and then ask permission to work with them. That's the ritual you see on the television shows."

"Ah, fascinating. I didn't think about the fact that you would work with other people's guides. Wait, so you mean we all have our own spirit guides?" Kane perked up as though she'd just told him he'd won a prize.

"Yes." Iris laughed at Kane's delighted look.

"No way. You mean I've got a pack of guides just hanging over my shoulder, likely shaking their heads at my poor excuse for work these days?" Kane asked.

"No, not like that." Iris surprised herself by giggling. She wasn't someone who giggled, at least not that she could recall. "They aren't there to judge you. A guide is meant to, well, guide you. If they just sat around and judged you all day, well, that probably wouldn't be very motivating, would it?"

"Oh, so they're like life coaches?" Kane asked.

"Something like that." Iris smiled, enjoying how his brain worked. She knew what was coming next but didn't mind. People always asked her to tell them about their spirit guides. Technically, it was a free reading, so she usually didn't do it. But with Kane, she wouldn't mind. He'd been very nice to her since they'd met.

"Again, fascinating. Do I just, like, give them a high five once in a while?" Kane mimicked high-fiving the air, and Iris collapsed in laughter. "Thank them for the help?"

"I'm sure they'd be delighted." Iris couldn't remember the last time she'd laughed this easily. "They do appreciate being acknowledged."

"You'll have to tell me how to do so. I can't believe how rude I've been all these years not to even say hello. It's properly un-Irish of me. We're known for our hospitality, you know," Kane said. He shook his head sadly as though he'd let all of Ireland down by not welcoming his spirit guides properly.

"Luckily, they're incredibly forgiving," Iris said and laughed when Kane mock wiped his brow.

"Have they given you any insight on what you've learned today? Would you consult them in matters like this? Or are they just sort of there on the back burner and available as needed?" Kane asked, surprising Iris by not asking more about himself. He was genuinely interested in *her*, it seemed.

"Ah, well. I don't know that my spirit guides are the same as others. Because of my ability, I have highly developed communication patterns with them. It wouldn't be the same for others. It's basically like turning the volume up, I suppose." Iris tapped a finger to her lips. "But yes, they've been chattering at me all day. It seems they're quite excited about me meeting up with Gracie, and they view this as a good development. I'm...I'm trying to listen to them more."

"Wait...you don't always listen to them? You, like, have a direct line to otherworldly assistance in your life, and you ignore it?" Kane looked at her with shock.

"Yes, okay, sometimes I ignore it, Judgey McJudgerson." Iris narrowed her eyes at Kane.

"Sorry, sorry, sorry. I realize now how that must have sounded." Kane held his hands up in the air.

"We all have free choice. Yes, I'm lucky to have guidance. But because I have so much of it, I don't know... sometimes...I guess I feel like I have to go against the guidance just to make sure my own voice doesn't get lost, if that makes sense?" Iris had never had to explain this to someone else before, and now she found herself struggling to put into words her need to still be independent of her spirit guides. Nobody had cared enough to ask her before, she realized, her eyes catching on Kane's. But this man? He truly was interested. Not just in her gift but in her.

"Ahhh, sure, sure," Kane said, nodding along. "It's like if my mam was muttering over my shoulder all the time. You still want to do your own thing."

"Something like that. Overall, I'm lucky for their support. They tried to warn me away from Warren, you know..." Iris sighed. "That was one area I should have listened to them in. Now, I'm trying to be better about doing so. I think I'm confident enough now in who I am as a person to know my own voice but give my guides more input in my life as well. That's why I accepted your offer for a ride, by the way."

"Is it? Well, I'll have to thank them." A confused look

crossed Kane's face, and he leaned forward. For a heart-stopping second, Iris thought he would kiss her, and warmth bloomed low in her stomach. "Can they hear me?" Kane whispered.

"Yes." Iris giggled again. Who was she? She never giggled.

"Ah, well, thank you, Iris's guides, for telling her to ride with me. I've really enjoyed getting to know her. You've got someone special on your hands. That's the truth of it." Kane spoke into the air over his head, not catching Iris's look of awe at his words. She'd composed herself by the time he looked back down, but the feeling of his words had imprinted on her heart. She studied him, curious now, and wondered...what-if?

Lara chattered in her ear, and Iris shook her head, tuning in to the spirit guide.

"He's a good one, Iris. Keep him."

Iris rolled her eyes and muted her.

"They say you're welcome," Iris said instead. She picked at a loose thread in the blanket and drained her wine.

"Shall we order pizza? I bet it will take a while to get here on a rainy night like tonight." Kane pulled out his phone, and Iris took that moment to study him. He hadn't asked about himself. Most people immediately wanted to know what their guides wanted them to know. But no, Kane had wanted to know how she handled things and then had thanked her guides for directing her to him. She realized he was working his way into her heart, and the thought made her decidedly uncomfortable. It was too soon, wasn't it? To have a crush on someone? She had trust issues a mile long. There was no reason for her to look at another man this way.

"Do you want anything special?"

"Three cheese for me," Iris said, laughing when Kane shook his head sadly.

"And here I thought I liked you, Iris."

"There's nothing wrong with simple," Iris protested. "Sometimes my life feels too complicated."

"Well, let's un-complicate things for the night, shall we?" Kane placed their order and then reached for the remote, flicking the television on. After twenty minutes of trying to figure out how to find the guide, in which Iris needled him endlessly, he landed on *Indiana Jones.* "How about this? It's that or a murder mystery."

"Let's do it," Iris said, smiling when Kane brought the wine bottle to her glass and topped her off. "I could use some action."

"Um…" Kane wiggled his eyebrows at her, though his eyes heated in his face. Iris laughed, but she caught on to his look, and the moment drew out. A knock sounded at the door, startling Iris, and she almost dropped her glass.

"Pizza!" Kane exclaimed.

The night flew by in a blur of laughter, pizza, and arguments over why Indiana Jones never listened to the smart women guiding him in his life. The hours drifted by and, for the first time, Iris didn't think about work or anything else. She just existed in the moment, enjoying spirited discussion about nonsense topics and even a third glass of wine.

"Iris," Kane whispered, his mouth near her face. Iris shifted and reached up, twining her arms around his neck, pulling his mouth to hers. Instantly, her body lit with need, and she dove her hands into his hair, sliding into the heat of his kiss. His lips tasted like wine, his mouth like sin, and liquid warmth slid through her body as she arched into him. Warren had never kissed like this. Kane's lips on hers ignited her whole body, and she wanted…

Wait. Iris pulled back and blinked at Kane in confusion, clearing her fuzzy brain. They were still on the couch, and Kane's eyes were heavy-lidded with need. He cleared his throat and eased gently back.

"You fell asleep…I was just waking you up to see if you wanted to take the guest bedroom…" Kane said, his voice a touch raspy.

Iris's body thrummed with need, and her chest rose steadily as she tried to control her breathing. She'd fallen *asleep*. Of course. And when Kane had woken her up, she'd automatically pulled him in for a kiss. Despite her tough demeanor, Iris loved to cuddle, so it wasn't uncommon for her to sleepily snuggle up to her partner. Now, realizing what had happened, embarrassment thrummed through her.

"Oh gosh, Kane, I'm sorry. I didn't even…" Iris shook her head, clearing the cobwebs.

"No, it's okay…it's fine. I know you weren't taking advantage of me," Kane said, a mocking note in his tone, cutting some of the tension with humor.

"Hard to do that when I'm dead asleep." Iris narrowed her eyes and sat up further on the couch. "Um, yeah. So. Well, you're a great kisser, by the way."

"Thanks." Kane mockingly patted himself on the back.

He hadn't moved back. Instead, they sat, both positioned on the precipice of something more, unsure of what to do.

"I...we probably shouldn't..." Iris began.

"Agreed. We're not..." Kane eased back immediately.

"Yeah, too soon. Breakups and all that..." Iris jumped in.

"Damaged goods. Trust issues," Kane agreed.

"So..." Iris looked at Kane. He was adorably rumpled in the way of someone just rolling from bed, and she wanted to run her hands through his hair once more. God, she wanted to jump him. Just crawl right on top of him, straddle him, and kiss him until she couldn't think straight. It was such an unusual impulse for her that Iris was certain it must be the wine at play.

"Just friends." Kane held out a hand.

"Just friends," Iris said, letting out a little sigh. They shook on it, their palms heating at the touch, and Iris wondered why she suddenly felt bereft. This was the right choice for both of them, and she'd already had a long week of emotional upheaval. It was likely that which was clouding her thoughts at the moment. Looking up at him, she smiled. "I'll take that guest bedroom. I'm about two seconds from falling back asleep."

It was a lie, of course, and Iris lay awake for another hour, detailing every moment of their kiss, deliberately keeping her spirit guides on mute.

She wasn't ready to hear what they had to say.

CHAPTER 12

ot once but twice the night before, Kane had gone and stood outside the guest room door, his hand poised to knock before he'd retreated. A part of him wished she'd never kissed him.

The other part would never forget it.

Her taste was imprinted on his soul now. The feel of her lips seared into his mind. It was as though Iris's kiss had thawed him, and now he was feeling…well, everything. Lust being at the forefront, naturally.

She'd kissed him like a long-lost lover coming home. His body had instantly responded, and he was certain he would have continued to the bedroom with her had she been up for it. Even if it wasn't the best choice for either of them at the moment, sometimes needs won out over rational thought.

But as soon as she'd pumped the brakes, Kane had followed suit. Iris wasn't wrong. They both were in a terrible position to be starting anything with someone else, particularly someone they both respected. Neither of them was interested in hurting the other. Instead, they had a nice friendship blooming.

And that is where it needed to stay.

Even though he'd pleasured himself twice to her image the night before.

Kane picked up his phone to text her, shaking his head at the memory, and wondered if she had similar confused feelings. He'd only dropped her off a few hours ago, noting that she was much like him and reluctant to speak before coffee in the morning.

> Kane: His father's betrayed him. Put his name out to the press with a contest stating that the first woman to get a proposal from his son gets a million dollars. Now his PR agent has to work even harder to protect him from the press or lose her job. They've gone to Scotland to hide.

> Iris: Why Scotland?

> Kane: The Highlands offer a lot of wide-open spaces with not a lot of paparazzi. I'm thinking it best to have them hole up in a one-bedroom cabin, though.

> Iris: I thought he was a rock star? Can't he afford a place with more than one bedroom?

> Kane: Can. But it would tip the press that someone rich and fancy is hiding out there.

> Iris: Ah, I see. So it's the "only one bed" trope. Does he offer her the bed?

Kane: Of course not, he's a rock star.

Iris: I don't like him.

Kane: But I have to make you hate him first to redeem himself. How will he do that?

Iris: Maybe he comes out in the middle of the night and sees her uncomfortable on the couch?

The text brought up how he'd felt last night when he'd woken her up, not wanting her to become stiff from lying in an awkward position, and she'd wound her arms around his neck. He realized he could use those emotions in his book, already jotting down notes on a notepad by his computer.

Kane: That'll do it.

Kane watched as the little bubbles of text typing showed up, then disappeared. He waited for her to write more. When nothing came, he wrote back.

Kane: Out with it.

Iris: Well, why is the dad putting a bet on his only son? And why doesn't the PR woman just pretend to be his fiancée then? Wouldn't that get people off his back and stop the dad in his weird contest?

All good points, Kane thought, jotting down her feedback. He would need to mull that storyline a bit but, if so, he could make it a forced proximity and a fake dating situation, which were fan favorites.

> Kane: I like how your brain works. I realize I didn't tell you about the will. There's more at play here forcing the father into doing this. It's a battle between father and son over who will get the record company. The stipulation in the will states the son has to marry Grandpa's chosen bride. If not, Daddy gets the company. And Daddy wants what he wants. Even if it means running over his son in the process.

> Iris: That's cold. So wait, we've got arranged marriage, potential fake dating, and forced proximity? And family betrayal? Okay, I'm intrigued.

> Kane: Thanks for your help. I can't tell you how delighted I am to be writing again. Catch up with you later. I'll let you know how it turns out.

> Iris: So you're just gonna leave me hanging?

> Kane: That's my job. We call those cliffhangers.

> Iris: Rude.

> Kane: I like to leave them wanting more.

> Iris: **middle finger emoji**

> Kane: **blows kisses**

There, Kane thought, pleased with the text interaction. They were on even ground again, having moved past the kiss, and she'd even placed some nuggets of the storyline in his brain for him to mine. Opening his computer, he pushed all thoughts of Iris aside and dove into his story with enthusiasm. Hours later, the buzzing of his phone finally pulled him from his work, though not without annoyance. Blinking at the screen, he saw several missed calls from his agent.

"What's up, man?" Kane asked, sighing as he rolled the tension out of his shoulders. Pushing back from the table, he stood and snagged his mug before walking to the kitchen to put the kettle on.

"I've been worried about you. You haven't been responding to emails," Grant said. A horn honked in the background, and Kane wondered if Grant conducted all of his phone calls while commuting instead of from his office.

"That would require me to sign into my emails. Which I haven't," Kane said cheerfully as he rinsed out his mug. "Because I've been writing."

"Finally!" In what Kane could only assume was gratitude, Grant swore profusely into the phone and then let out a whoop. "I've been waiting to hear this. I'm really happy for you, man. In that case, um, best not to open your email then."

Kane stilled. Closing his eyes, he took a deep breath. Of course he'd open his email now that Grant had put this in his head.

"Just tell me," Kane ordered.

"Ah, well, you probably won't be much bothered. But

I'd rather you hear it from me than someone else," Grant began.

"And by hearing it from you…you mean in an email? Is that how you break news to me?" Kane asked. He was already across the room and back at his makeshift desk. Clicking out of his manuscript, he opened his email box.

"Well, yes, this news. Because, if you'll notice, you've ignored my last like thirty calls. Plus, since it was a news piece, I figured it best to just send the article along. Either way, let me rip the Band-Aid off. Alison got married."

"My…wait, already?" Kane's mouth dropped open. He clicked on Grant's email and immediately on the link to the news article. At the top of the article was a photo of a beaming Alison next to the man who had edited every one of his best-selling books. Alison looked beautiful in a classic white dress, with white flowers, in a white-on-white reception hall.

Did she really get to use all white when she'd cheated with her now-husband? It wasn't exactly what one would call a pure start to the relationship, was it? Kane sniffed, annoyed at his thoughts. Alison had been a mistake he shouldn't have made, yet this news article still rankled. Maybe it was because of how quickly she'd moved on.

Well, she'd moved on before the end of their relationship, hadn't she? Either way, Kane couldn't help but feel like a fool. He didn't want to be the person who begrudged someone else their happiness. Still, he was having a tough time thinking any kind thoughts toward the happy couple at the moment.

And frankly, good editors were hard to find.

Shoving back, he tuned in to Grant's voice.

"You okay, man? Sorry to be the bearer of bad news," Grant said.

"It's not bad. It's just annoying, is what it is. Like… what was the rush? She'd already been awful to me. It's like adding insult to injury," Kane said.

"Cheaters often do that, you know. It validates the cheating. That way, they can say they cheated out of finding true love and all that bullshit. Trust me, I know it," Grant seethed. He did, at that. While Grant could be a jerk, a cheater he was not. Kane had been through a few divorces with Grant to know the man's views on liars and cheats. He might not be an easy husband, but he wasn't one to lie to his wives. It was another reason Kane continued working with the notoriously difficult agent. Under the tough exterior lay a good heart.

"Thanks for telling me," Kane said. He sighed and went back to the kitchen to pour the boiling water over a tea bag in his mug. "It is what it is."

"Tell me about the story." Grant switched subjects, and Kane was grateful for it. They spent the next twenty minutes kicking around more story ideas, and then Kane hung up. Suddenly, he felt deeply drained, as though he'd run a marathon, and he dropped onto the couch and stared out at the misty rain that blanketed the harbor.

For a moment, he just dropped his face into his hands and breathed, trying to get a read on his feelings. He didn't miss Alison. But he did miss being in a relationship. He spent so much time alone in his thoughts during the day that he missed the companionship of having someone to speak to when he finished work. Even if Alison had been the wrong partner for him, something he'd come to realize over the past few months, what she had done to him still hurt.

Betrayal hurt. Pure and simple.

His phone buzzed with a text message.

> Iris: What's wrong?

> Kane: What do you mean?

> Iris: My spirit guides just told me something's wrong with you. Are you okay? Did you hurt yourself?

> Kane: Wow, that's...trippy.

> Iris: Sorry, am I intruding? It kind of comes with the territory with me. I forgot to explain that. Once you're my friend, I can't help but look out for you.

Kane looked at his phone for a moment, measuring the pros and cons of telling Iris why he was bummed out. However, she was a woman who understood betrayal. He might as well talk to someone about it.

> Kane: My ex just got married. A friend told me and sent me a photo.

> Iris: Oof. Already? That seems...

> Kane: Fast? Rude? Annoying? Yes, all of those things.

> Iris: What did she wear?

> Kane: What do you mean, what did she wear? A simple white dress. And white flowers. And white everything.

> Iris: Yawn.

Kane cracked up and leaned back against the couch, Iris's comment loosening a knot in his chest.

> Kane: Not an all-white girl, are ya?

> Iris: Not likely, no. Maybe I would be…if I could wear my purple boots. They complete me in ways that nobody has before.

> Kane: Should I be jealous of a pair of boots?

> Iris: You should be. They're really excellent boots. They support me, make me smile, are comfortable to be with, and make me feel pretty. You know what? I think I'm in a relationship with my boots.

Kane's lips quirked. The tension that had formed in his stomach eased and he relaxed into the cushions, kicking his feet up on the couch.

> Kane: Tell me more. **Heavy breathing.**

> Iris: Oooh, does the man have a thing for leather? Or is it the shoes…wait, is it a foot thing? Are you a foot guy? Can I sell you photos of my feet? Maybe that's a new career path that I've yet to explore. Hmm…

> Kane: I hear those models get shoes purchased by their admirers. I bet you'd get all the boots you wanted.

> Iris: And cheat on my purple boots?
> What kind of woman do you think I am?!

> Kane: You're right, you're right. My
> apologies. I should know better.

> Iris: Do you need to go for a drink or
> something? Cry on my shoulder? Hit on
> women? I'm a great wingwoman. Tell me
> what you need.

Kane considered it for a moment but realized his long hours of creating plus the news of Alison's marriage had left him drained. He wanted nothing more than to pull the throw blanket over his head and take a long nap.

> Kane: I'm good. I have a date with my
> couch.

> Iris: Oohhh, you're also dating an
> inanimate object. I like that about you,
> Kane.

Kane snickered, appreciating her wicked sense of humor.

> Kane: Thanks, though. Seriously. I feel
> better. Catch up with you later.

> Iris: Sleep well. Wink. **heavy breathing
> noises.**

> Kane: Jerk.

This time, when he settled back into the cushions and closed his eyes, an easy smile hovered on his lips.

CHAPTER 13

For Rent.

Iris stopped in her tracks, her pulse picking up as she studied the sign hanging in the glass window of a door painted a bright purple color, almost the exact shade of her boots. She wasn't sure if it was the door's color or the sign that stopped her, but now it seemed almost serendipitous as she turned and scanned the corner location on a bustling street near the harbor. One narrow window showed a sliver of a larger room, and the lack of more windows was a plus, at least for Iris's business. She'd found that her clientele preferred discretion during their readings, and nobody enjoyed having pedestrians peek in on their most vulnerable moments.

Pursing her lips, Iris stepped back and studied the two-story building. The first floor seemed to consist of two shops, the other being a bookstore. She guessed the second floor had apartments, based on the cat sitting in one of the windows next to a few potted plants. Testing her emotions, Iris discovered that the location felt…good.

It felt right.

Before she could talk herself out of taking the leap, Iris pulled out her phone and dialed the number listed on the sign outside.

"Hello, yes, I just noticed the sign on the shop door? I'm interested in learning more about the property." Iris paused when the door of the bookshop next door opened, and a woman popped her head out. In her late sixties with a crop of shaggy white hair and beaming blue eyes, she held the phone to her ear as she scanned the street until her eyes landed on Iris.

"Are you calling about the shop?" the woman asked.

"That's me," Iris said with a smile. She disconnected and walked closer to the woman.

"My name is Beatrice. I own the building, making it easy to give a tour if needed. Let me just lock up, and I'll be showing you the place then," Beatrice said. She was gone before Iris could say anything else. She'd just wanted to know the shop's price, and now it seemed she was stuck with a tour. It couldn't hurt, she supposed, to just take a peek inside and test how she felt about starting up another shop.

It had been a few days since Gracie had dropped the bombshell on her about having family here. In that time, Gracie had made good on her word. She'd shown up every day, obnoxiously towing Iris around the village and introducing her to everyone. It turned out that Gracie hadn't been lying. There were many free-spirited and magickal women in this town so, instead of feeling like she had to hide who she was, Iris was placed in the odd position of quickly gaining a small army of women determined to protect her reputation. It seemed the battle cry had gone up once Gracie had learned who Iris was and what she was dealing with back home, and now various revenge plots were being hatched. At this point, Iris almost felt bad for Warren. She suspected his life would not go very smoothly for that much longer.

She was also struggling with wrapping her head around the concept of family. It had just been her and her mother for so long that having what kind of felt like a group of sisters was...daunting. She'd met Gracie, Kira, and Fi. Supposedly, Niamh and Mac, her actual cousin, were meant to be heading to Grace's Cove soon. But the other three women, who chattered incessantly, talking over each other and nosing in each other's business, were more than enough for Iris to contend with. It felt a bit like being descended upon by a group of cheerful fairies, each buzzing about and confident in their own power. She hoped that one day she'd feel more comfortable with them but, for now, Iris had done her best to engage, but with caution. She needed to keep her walls up right now, as that was the only thing protecting her from more hurt.

She did stupid things when her walls came down, like kiss Kane. Iris absentmindedly rubbed her lips while she waited for Beatrice to grab a key and lock up the bookstore. She'd replayed the kiss more times than she should have for someone who had insisted they remain friends. Intellectually, she knew that being friends was the smart choice.

Emotionally? She wanted to give in to lust and pounce on the man. He would be fun, she'd realized. Just a ton of fun to roll around with in bed and then watch old movies together over pizza. It was the simple things that made for an ideal relationship, and she'd never really had that connection with Warren. But now, as she bantered back and forth with Kane over this script he was writing, she found herself looking forward to his messages each day.

In a friendly way, of course.

She also kind of wanted to know what happened next in his story. It was right up her alley, what with the rock stars, family betrayal, and a juicy good love story mixed in. She liked to decompress with those kinds of books after a long day of managing people's emotions.

"Here we are. Sorry about that. I thought I'd hung them back up after the last person toured it," Beatrice said. She brandished a key gleefully in front of her.

"Have you had a lot of interest in the property?" Iris asked, worry flashing through her. Which wasn't a good sign. Because she was *just* looking, she lectured herself as she held the door open for Beatrice after the woman had unlocked it.

"Oh, several have come through. I just put up the sign yesterday. I didn't catch your name, dear?" Beatrice asked. She tugged lightly at the curtain on the window, pulling it back to let more light spill into the space.

"Iris. It's nice to meet you," Iris said, devouring the shop. It was just...well, it was perfect. The track lighting in the ceiling offered enough light that it wouldn't feel gloomy inside with the curtain pulled closed over the window, and the honey-colored wood floors gleamed. It was a simple open room, with a long counter on the back wall situated in front of a row of cupboards. There were two doors on the back wall, one which led to a small bathroom and another to a tiny kitchenette and storage area. Two of the long walls were a lovely red brick, and the main wall separating the shop from the stairwell that ran upstairs was painted a soft mossy green.

Immediately, Iris pictured throwing down some colorful rugs and adding a few comfortable chairs to create a welcoming space for people. Perhaps some art from Aislinn's gallery on the wall to add some ambience to the room. She didn't need much to do her work, but it was more about creating a client experience that met their expectations. She liked to provide a professional atmosphere with just enough woo-woo so people also got the excitement of visiting a psychic. It was kind of like mixing a doctor's waiting room with a theme park.

"The apartment upstairs is available as well and can be included in the package for rent."

"Is that right?" Iris turned to Beatrice. "Is it available to look at?"

"It is. The last tenant lived above and ran her shop. It's an easy commute to work. I live in the other apartment with my cat, Bubbles. I'd prefer a neighbor that isn't too noisy, though I've been known to party it up on occasion myself." Beatrice winked at her, and Iris laughed. She followed the woman from the front door, waiting while she locked the shop door, and then pushed through the doorway that led to a set of stairs that ran directly up to a landing with a door on either side. Sliding the key in the lock, Beatrice pushed the door open.

"I just had it cleaned, so it should be ready to move in. The last tenant was very clean and didn't make many changes to the flat. Though you're fine to change the paint color if needed." Beatrice stepped back and waited as Iris stepped inside. The layout was much the same as the shop below, except the apartment was divided into a living area with a kitchen and a separate bedroom with a serviceable en suite bathroom. But the windows at the front of the living area drew Iris. They stretched up to the high ceilings, creating an illusion of more space, and offered a stunning view of the water and the bustling village street below. Immediately charmed, Iris was already picturing how she would make the space home.

And just what did that say about her decision to stay?

"There's also a small balcony out of this door here if you like to sit outside." Beatrice pointed at a door by the kitchen.

"Beatrice, this is all lovely. What is the monthly rent for both?"

Beatrice quoted a number that had Iris beaming. She was used to Boston prices, so this positively felt like a steal. Granted, she'd had a lot more business in Boston. That being said, as John had reminded her over and over since she'd arrived, her nest egg was quite large. She could afford to make these types of decisions if she wanted to.

"I…" Iris hesitated. She'd need to tell this bright-eyed woman what she did for a living. Not only could Iris tell that she was the type of sweet-hearted woman who would likely lend her books and bring her baked goods, but she also didn't want to deal with someone who would try to oust her if they disagreed with her choice of profession. People had varying reactions to psychics, and Iris found it usually best to be upfront.

"Oh, do you hear Bubbles? She hears us. Do you like

cats?" Beatrice trilled, leaving the door open and walking across the landing. There, she unlocked her door, and a fat orange cat scampered out straight to where Iris stood at the front windows.

"Hi, Bubbles," Iris said, leaning down.

"Don't…well, then," Beatrice said, a note of surprise in her words.

"She's very sweet," Iris said, running her hand down the cat's back.

"Usually, she doesn't take to people that quickly. She's a bit standoffish, which I don't mind. I consider her to be a good judge of character," Beatrice said.

"Is that right? I can be a bit standoffish as well." Iris chuckled and straightened. "Beatrice, I love both properties, and I'd like to rent them from you. But full disclosure. I'm a psychic medium, so I'll be doing readings for clients who need guidance. Is that something that you are comfortable with?"

"Will you be working with any bad spirits? Inviting any nasty things into the house?" Beatrice narrowed her eyes at Iris.

"Nope, nothing like that. There are no rituals. No magick. No spells. I just close my eyes and tune into the spirit guides. They answer questions for my clients. I help guide them in whatever's bothering them at the moment."

"Hmm, like a counselor, but like…enhanced. With spiritual guidance."

"Yes, but not like…religious," Iris hastened to clarify. That could always be a tricky area for some people. Iris didn't believe in any one religion, nor did she need to. She already understood more about love, oneness, and universal energy than most people ever would in their lifetime.

"Well, sure, and I can be understanding that. I read a lot, you know." Beatrice tapped a finger to her wrinkled forehead. "I have a deep thirst for knowledge. Your profession doesn't bother me, Iris, if that's what you're worried about."

"I just wanted to make sure. You seem very nice, and I would hate for you to get upset about my shop once I open up," Iris said. A trickle of excitement went through her at the thought of opening her own shop. The last place she'd opened had been with the help of Warren. A lot of her decisions had been overridden by his choices, and now the thought of being able to make a space thoroughly and completely hers lit her up inside.

Perhaps Gracie was right–maybe Iris *could* have a fresh start here. Granted, she'd need to look into all the paperwork regarding getting a visa and establishing her residency, but Dylan had already assured her that he could help in that department.

Now, she just had to decide if she was ready to make the leap.

Bubbles bumped her head against Iris's leg, her purr sounding like a little motor, her tail making spiky little movements in the air. It was as though she was nudging Iris to make the right decision.

"I'll take it. When can I move in?"

"As soon as the money's transferred and the contract is signed, you can move in whenever," Beatrice beamed at her. "Welcome home, neighbor."

Her spirit guides cheered in her head, and Iris realized

that she'd made the decision without consulting them. Maybe, just maybe, Iris could find a happy medium between trusting her gut and listening to her guides for support. It seemed like today may have been the first step in the right direction.

And a new life for Iris.

She wanted to tell Kane. Iris wondered what he would think about her opening her own place and if he'd want to help her set the shop up. Then she paused, still petting Bubbles, and realized she'd already defaulted to wanting to tell a man about her own professional choices.

No, not this time.

This time Iris was going to do things on her own.

And in exactly the way that she wanted to. Resolved, she grinned down at Bubbles.

"Looks like I'll need to start stocking kitty treats."

"Like she needs any more," Beatrice said. "Don't look at me like that, Bubbles. You're overfed as it is."

CHAPTER 14

$\mathcal{I}$t had been over a week since Kane had last seen Iris, though they'd spoken almost constantly over text messages. Kane had to admit he'd enjoyed their daily banter, and her unique outlook on life was helping him work through his writing blocks.

Kane hadn't even thought about Alison getting married.

It was strange, wasn't it, that a woman he had once thought he'd spend his life with hadn't entered his thoughts at all since Iris had helped him to release whatever tension he'd held around the situation. Grant had been helpful in hooking him up with several new potential editors, and he'd enjoyed interviewing the candidates. Frankly, he'd vibed with one guy so quickly that he was almost grateful to Alison for stealing his original editor. Kane felt that this new editor would bring a wealth of fresh insights into his work–which was exactly what he needed to grow as a writer. However, after a long week at his computer, Kane was ready to step away and take a break.

Kane wondered if Iris would be willing to join him for a pint later so he could catch up with her in person. She'd been working on a special project this week that she refused to tell him about, though he was determined to pull it out of her.

Kane: It's a strip club, isn't it?

Iris: You wish. Actually, you probably don't. If I opened a strip club, it would be an all-male review.

Kane: Those guys are intimidating. They are hairless and tanned and way too muscular. How do they even look like that?

Iris: They eat air and live in the gym.

Kane: That's certainly a choice. Speaking of choices, would you choose to join me for a pint later? My eyes are starting to burn after sitting at this computer all week. I should probably surface and interact with humans again.

Iris: Yeah, I think that would work. How's the story coming along?

Kane: Well, I've got my couple stuck in their cottage in Scotland. He's furious at his father, mad at the world for intruding on his privacy, and annoyed that the PR company has sent a handler to manage him. She's trying to remind herself that she desperately needs the money to one day leave the PR agency and pursue her dream of becoming a singer/songwriter someday.

Iris: Ohhhh, she's a budding songwriter? The plot thickens. Does rock star know this about her yet?

Kane: No, she's keeping it from him because she's starting to see past his grumpy exterior and how the whole world uses him. She refuses to do the same.

Iris: I like her. Plucky. Wants to make it on her own merits, right?"

Kane: Exactly. Then he slips out for a night at the pub because he can't stay holed up in the cabin anymore and is immediately recognized. Gets swamped by women.

Iris: Ohhh, and she'll have to rescue him, won't she? Is this where he'll tell the world he already picked a woman? And pretend it's her?

Kane: I think so, but I still need to work through it. We can't forget the arranged marriage from his grandfather either. We don't know who that woman is yet.

Iris: Hmm, could be a love triangle there. Tell me more…

Kane: There is no more. I'm still working it out.

Iris: Work faster.

Kane: You're a cruel taskmaster, Iris. Take pity on my poor, tired brain.

Iris: I'll allow you a break tonight, then.
See you later.

Kane smiled, pleased that he would see her later, and then stretched. He needed to do some basic adulting, or they'd have to shovel him out of the mess of his house. Putting on some music, Kane sang along to Pearl Jam as he cleaned the cottage, took out the trash, and put the laundry on. Then once he'd changed his sheets and finished tidying up, he took a long, hot shower. The water warmed his aching shoulder muscles, a product of too much time hunched over the computer, and he relaxed against the wall. Once again, his thoughts strayed to Iris, and he found himself thinking about their kiss for the thousandth time that week. His body responded to the memory, and Kane groaned, finding himself with his hand, and he worked the lust from his body. He'd done this more times than he'd like to admit, each time pleasuring himself to the memory of how Iris had made him feel.

With one kiss, she'd unlocked something inside him that had been dormant for much too long. Longer than before Alison had left him, stunned, at the altar. It was like he'd been living in black and white, and Iris came along with her purple boots and kicked down the door to his emotions. Now, he wanted a taste of her again more than anything else.

But she'd told him no. And he would respect that because that was the kind of man Kane was. However, he wasn't above looking for any opening that she would give him. If their banter turned flirty again, Kane planned to lean into it. It was hard to say where their friendship would lead, but he wasn't going to put what they had into a box. Instead, Kane planned to wait and see, patiently biding his time until she let him in for a kiss once more.

And if she didn't, well, he'd have to make peace with that as well. She'd already given him a big gift by helping him break through an emotional career block and, for that alone, he'd forever be grateful.

But...her mouth.

He could just imagine that luscious mouth of hers on him, and Kane groaned as he finished, banging his forehead lightly against the shower wall, the warm water streaming down his back.

Yeah, he had it bad for Iris.

Later, after Kane had completed his chores and felt like a functioning adult with a clean house and laundry finished, he went out for the last of his daily chores–groceries. Whistling, he drove into town and found a spot by the water. He could wander down the street and stop at the bakery, liquor store, and supermarket. It was a nicer day, as the weather went in Ireland, with only a touch of chill on the wind and a few dim rays of sunshine poking through the gray clouds. Kane pulled his cap a little farther down on his head and turned a corner just in time to hear a curse.

"Blasted stupid table."

"Iris, what are you doing?" Kane laughed at Iris, who stood on the sidewalk next to a large wooden dining table.

"Oh, Kane, hi." Iris glanced at him, frustration clear on her face. "Um, just trying to move this table. It's fine, just will take a moment is all."

"Where are you trying to move it? Back to your place?

I can help," Kane said. He shook his head at her. Clearly, this was a two-person job. Stubborn woman.

"Um, well, inside here. Actually." An unreadable look crossed Iris's face, and Kane glanced over her shoulder to the store behind her.

"Why are you trying to move a table into someone's store, Iris? Shouldn't the owner be helping you?" Kane asked, forcing her to meet his eyes.

"It's…" Iris mumbled something, and he leaned closer.

"Did you forget how to speak, Iris?"

"It's my store, okay? Mine. I rented it. I know it's crazy, and I'm probably going to lose a boatload of money, and nobody's going to come for a reading. Still, I'm doing it, okay?" Iris's eyes blazed in her face when she looked up at Kane and he realized that his prickly tough friend might be dangerously close to tears.

"Well, honestly, I'm surprised it took you this long," Kane said with a shrug. He picked up one end of the table with his back to the store so Iris could direct him and arched a brow at her. "Go on then, don't be stubborn. Let's get this table inside before the rain comes."

"It's not going to rain. I can do this myself. It just… takes longer," Iris argued, her hands on her hips.

A few rain droplets spat out of the clouds above her head, and Iris glared at the sky. Kane's lips quirked.

"It always rains in Ireland, darling. Come on, then, no time left to argue. We'll get this sorted quickly, and you'll have your table," Kane said. He lifted his side of the table, and Iris finally gave in, quickly directing him up the steps. They pivoted through the doorway, angling the table so it would fit. Kane barely resisted screaming, "Pivot!" loudly in case Iris had never seen that *Friends* episode. She'd already told him that she didn't watch much television, and he didn't want to look silly in front of her.

"I think...back here," Iris said, nodding toward the back of the room. Kane dutifully walked backward until the table sat to the side of a check-out counter in front of the cupboards. Brushing off his hands, he turned and scanned the place. The space had potential with high ceilings, soft lighting, and pretty wood floors. Turning, he beamed at Iris.

"I love this spot," Kane said.

"Do you? I...well, I guess it spoke to me. I don't know...I don't know what I'm doing," Iris said, crossing her arms over her chest and worrying her bottom lip with her teeth. Kane's eyes caught on her mouth, and he needed to pull his gaze away before he got himself worked up again.

"I find that hard to believe," Kane said, keeping his tone light.

"Really? Why?" Iris demanded, her eyes huge in her face.

"Because I think you're capable of making anything you do a success." Kane shrugged and turned to look at the room again. "This is a nice space in a great village, where it sounds like you might have a bit of a support network. Whatever you do here is likely going to do well. And it's not as huge a risk as you think–so long as you're not breaking the bank to start this. Is it...will you be doing readings again? Or are you starting something else?"

"Readings," Iris admitted, a guilty look flashing across her face. "I know that I probably shouldn't, what with everything that's going on in the press. But…I love it, and it's who I am."

Kane hated seeing the doubt on her face. Thus far, she'd struck him as someone who could stand up for herself and speak her mind. Seeing this side of her made him want to protect her. It wasn't easy for a strong woman, well, any strong person really, to show their vulnerable side. Without thinking, he crossed to Iris and pulled her into his arms for a hug.

"Hey, listen to me," Kane said, pulling back a little so she could tilt her face up to look at him. He loved how she felt in his arms, and being this close to her made him even more acutely aware of their height difference. "You do not have to explain why you're opening another shop to anyone. Nor do you have to feel guilty. The only person who should feel guilty is that asshole of an ex-boyfriend who lied about you to the press. You've done nothing wrong, and if this genuinely brings you joy, well, you should embrace it. In fact, I think it's the smartest thing you can do."

"Really?" Light bloomed in Iris's eyes as she looked up at him.

"Sure, and I do. See, it's like falling off your bike, right? If you wait too long to get back on and try it again, well, it builds up to something bigger and bigger in your mind and, soon, you become too scared to try again. No, this makes perfect sense. Get on with it, and you'll be the better for it. I one hundred percent think this is the perfect choice for you."

Plus, it keeps you here in Ireland, Kane added silently.

"I…" Before Kane even grasped what was happening,

Iris's lips were on his. But once he realized it, he wouldn't miss this opportunity. He'd been craving a taste of her again, and now she'd given it to him. He angled his lips, deepening their kiss, and Iris moaned softly into his mouth.

It was the moan that undid him.

Scooping Iris up to sit on the table they'd just brought in, Kane nudged her legs open so he fit between them. He pressed against her, feeling how hard he was for her already, and heat licked low in his belly. Her kiss whispered a promise of something more to him, and now he didn't want to stop.

"I need more," Kane murmured against her lips, pulling back so he could trail kisses down her neck. Finding her collarbone, he nibbled lightly there, his hands stroking her sides as he waited to see what Iris would do. He knew she was gun-shy from her last relationship, but there was no way that she couldn't feel the energy that zipped between them. He'd felt it since the moment he'd shaken her hand in the airport two weeks ago.

He felt it every time he opened a door for her, and she brushed close to him.

He felt it when she shoved him good-naturedly when he said something that made her laugh.

He felt it when she'd kissed him the first time, her eyes sleepy and full of need.

And he felt it now, at this moment, wanting her more than anything else he'd wanted in...well, ever, really. Every text message this week had felt like a strange foreplay, where they built up each other's estimation of each other. He was a cerebral sort, and nothing was sexier than a woman who could banter ideas back and forth with him.

But as much as he wanted to take her, right here and right now, bending her over the table and sliding deep inside her until he eradicated all thoughts of another man from her mind, Kane knew he had to proceed cautiously.

Because the other thing was–she *had* become his friend. Perhaps, even annoyingly so. Which meant he had to treasure the friendship because no matter what happened between them, Kane realized he didn't want to lose Iris from his life.

"What…how…much more?" Iris gasped. He wondered if she even realized she was rubbing against him, thrusting her hips gently as he held her locked against his body.

"I want it all, Iris." Her eyes widened with shock, and he gave her a wicked smile that had pink flooding her cheeks. "But I'll take whatever you offer."

"Oh…my. Um…" Iris nibbled that delicious lower lip of hers again and stroked her hands up and down his chest, muttering to herself as she did so. He wondered if she consulted her spirit guides or was just caught up in her indecision. Helpless not to kiss her again while she mulled over what to do, he leaned over and bit her lower lip, sucking gently to take away the sting. "Ohhhhh."

Here was need and something more. Kane felt it as she wrapped her arms around his waist, pulling him tight so she all but rode him as their tongues twined together. Here was a match, two souls finding their twin, and he knew he'd need to show her what a relationship with a good man could look like.

"Okay, a *little* bit more…" Iris breathed against his

mouth, and Kane smiled. So he would take her, inch by impossible inch, toward the finish line that he could already envision. Maybe it was because he wrote romance novels, maybe it was because she had awoken something in him again, or maybe it was just because it was Iris. But the switch had flipped for him, and now he knew he had to make her see what could be.

So if it was to be a dance, then, well, he'd happily lead.

"Just a little bit then," Kane agreed, breathing softly at her lips, keeping his kiss gentle as he positioned his hands under her bum. Pulling her as tightly against him as he could, he began to meet her thrusting, rubbing himself against her, enjoying how she bowed backward with a soft moan, exposing the length of her throat. There, he kissed his way down her soft skin, loving how she shivered at his touch and reached for the first button on her oversized shirt. Gently, he unbuttoned her shirt until he revealed a simple tank bra in petal pink. Already Kane could see how her nipples stood at attention through the thin material, and he brushed his thumbs gently over them.

"Yes," Iris breathed, and Kane smiled, appreciating how responsive she was to the lightest of touches. He suspected she would be an active and willing participant in bed when he finally got her there. But not now, not today. This moment was just for her as he took her through the first steps of the dance they now found themselves in. Her breasts were lovely, round, and firm, and he cupped both in his hands, sliding the tank bra down to reveal creamy white skin and perfectly pink nipples.

He wanted to take each nipple in his mouth and see how she responded to his touch, but already she'd increased her rhythm against him. He wondered if she could come this way, riding him through his pants while his hands massaged her breasts. If he kissed her where he wanted to, he'd have to break contact with where she was pressed so tightly against him, and he refused to do that. Instead, he caressed her breasts, noting when she shivered, and increased his pace, thrusting harder against her.

"That's it, baby," Kane said, his breath hot at her ear. "I want you to come for me right now while you ride me. I want you to think about how amazing it would feel if I slid inside you right now, filling you, your body clenching around me as I thrust into you, over and over, so hot, so wet…yes, just like that."

When Iris arched against him, her legs trembling, he brought his lips to her mouth, capturing her cries as she came undone around him. He could have followed suit, he was that close but, luckily, he'd taken care of himself in the shower that morning and still held on to the tiniest thread of control. Instead, he stroked her back, holding her close to him, as she buried her head against his chest.

"That was…I don't even know what that was," Iris admitted.

Kane beamed at the top of her head, appreciating and understanding her shyness at the moment. It had been incredibly erotic to be able to touch her yet not touch her the way he wanted to, in this empty shop while the world passed by outside. Remembering the front window a touch too late, Kane glanced guiltily over his shoulder and was relieved to find the curtain was tugged closed across the window. That could have been bad for business, and he could kick himself for not checking that sooner.

"Incredible?" Kane supplied, pulling back and using a finger to tilt her chin up to look at him. "Super hot? Achingly erotic? Sexy enough to make me have naughty dreams for weeks?"

"You think I'm sexy?" Iris blinked up at him, and he laughed, surprised that was the point she would fixate on.

"I just dry-humped you into oblivion because that was the closest I could get to you. And I'd do it a hundred times over if it meant I got to have my hands on you. Sexy does not begin to describe what I think about you, Iris."

"Oh, my." Iris fanned her face, and Kane laughed, easing back a bit. He could see the moment she remembered that she thought she wasn't ready for a relationship. "Listen, Kane."

"Just friends," Kane said, tapping her nose. "Yup, I got it."

"Right, just friends. This was just…" Iris searched for the word. She looked cute, her hair rumpled, her delicious breasts still fully on display for Kane to enjoy. "An anomaly."

"An anomaly is something that deviates from the norm," Kane said, reaching over to twine a lock of her hair around his finger. "Wouldn't you say that we, as the people we are, already do that?"

"Well, sure, but I mean, like…for us. As friends. Friends aren't meant to do…that. Even oddball friends like us," Iris argued.

"And I'd disagree. I think the best relationships are ones where there's also a friendship, don't you?"

"I…" Iris scrunched her nose, caught.

"Is there any other heavy lifting you need me to do at

the moment?" Kane asked, brushing a kiss across her lips before she could jump back.

"No, I'm good," Iris said faintly.

"Great, then I'm off to the market. I'll see you for a pint later, then," Kane called, already at the door before she could cancel their plans for later. Which he knew she was going to try to do because once she got in that pretty head of hers and overanalyzed what had just happened, she would pull back from him. Instead, he gave her no chance to cancel and zipped out the door.

He almost stumbled over an old woman with bright eyes and a beaming smile.

"Well, hello there. I haven't met you yet. Are you a friend of Iris's?" she asked.

"Oh, I am. The *best* kind of friend," Kane clarified with a laugh.

"That's good, dear. We all need *those* kinds of friends." The woman winked at him and returned to the bookshop across from Iris's store.

Kane laughed the whole way to the market. He couldn't remember the last time he'd looked forward to an evening more.

CHAPTER 15

"*I*'m sorry, what now?" John asked, and Iris could hear him turning down the music playing in the background. "There must be a poor connection because I could have sworn you just said that hunky airport guy got you off on a dining room table."

"Ew, must you be so crude?" Iris closed her eyes.

"Yes, I must. Have you met me?" John demanded. "I need more details."

"I gave you the gist of it. Or thrust of it, if you must…" Iris groaned at her pun, but John laughed.

"I'm loving this. I am here for this. I am *living* for this," John exclaimed, and Iris winced, berating herself for telling him. Because now it was a thing. It didn't need to be a thing, right?

"I never should have told you," Iris groaned, flopping back on her bed, where she'd strewn what little clothes she had across the comforter.

"Yes, you should have. Because you need someone to talk you out of running away from Hottie McIrish."

"You don't even know what he looks like," Iris protested. She stared at the ceiling and brought Kane's face to her mind. Yeah, okay, he was hot.

"I don't need to. I can picture him perfectly. Now, when do you see him next?"

"Tonight," Iris whispered, nerves swirling in her stomach.

"Even better. What are you wearing?" John demanded.

"I don't know. I've pulled out every piece of clothing I brought with me." Iris sighed and wiped a hand over her face. "It's just a friend's thing. Not a date. We're just friends, John."

"Friends who touch each other's private parts. Got it," John said, humming. She could just see him tapping a finger to his lips, dressed crisply in a business suit, at his standing desk in his office.

"Dark jeans," John said.

"Got 'em." Iris 'blew out a breath, relieved he wasn't forcing her into a dress. Not that she had one but, knowing John, he'd have her out the door to shops if that was what he wanted for her.

"Just friends, you say, which we both know is a lie, but let's see. You don't want to look like you are trying too hard. Where are you going? An Irish pub?"

"Aren't all pubs in Ireland technically Irish?" Iris wondered.

"Shut it. Did you bring that deep-blue scoop-neck sweater I bought you?"

"Yes, I have it." Iris pulled it from the pile.

"Wear that with your dark jeans, hair loose, and big earrings. No necklaces. The scoop shows a lot of skin, so it's sexy but casual. And not your godawful tank bra. Something with some lift." John sniffed.

"It's terrifying that you know what underwear I prefer," Iris muttered.

"And not the purple boots. I know you love them, but they clash with the sweater. Did you bring those black booties? The ones with a bit of heel?"

"I did." Iris sighed, looking longingly at her purple boots.

"You can deal with them for a night, Iris. You wouldn't have called me if you didn't care how you looked. Now, I'll need a full report tomorrow. I have to hop on a call. Byeeeeee."

Best friends could be annoying, Iris thought, but at the same time–he wasn't wrong. She did care how she looked. Clothes could be armor, and she would need it when she faced Kane.

Had she really wrapped her legs around his waist and rode him like...like she had no self-control at all? Iris blushed at the memory, pulling a pillow over her face and screaming into it. This...this was not a woman she knew. She'd never done something so depraved in her life before.

"It's about time you started," Ophelia said in her mind.

"Oh wow, okay. So now my spirit guides are chiming in on my sex life too? Cool," Iris complained.

"We celebrate love in all its forms," Ophelia reminded her. She sounded prim, if an ethereal spirit being could be prim.

"News flash, it's not love," Iris said and muted Ophelia.

An hour later, Iris strolled into Gallagher's Pub in her

pre-approved outfit and had to admit that John knew what he was talking about. The color of the shirt popped her eyes and worked with her newly colored red hair, and the scoop neck was just low enough to be sexy without making her feel like she had to tug the neckline up every ten minutes. She'd thrown on some large gold hoop earrings and had lovingly waved goodbye to her purple boots before leaving the apartment. If things went well, she'd be in her new place by next week – pending the delivery of a new mattress.

The rush of images and voices that greeted her whenever she walked into a packed restaurant always gave her pause as spirits clamored to speak with her to reach their loved ones. Years ago, Iris would take the time to greet the guides and ascertain if she needed to approach someone with the information they wanted to pass on – to mixed results. After one too many times when a person had left visibly upset, Iris had stopped doing that. She would only approach a stranger and offer her insight in extreme cases. Still, it always took her a moment to steady herself and add an extra layer of noise protection, so to speak, in her mind before she was comfortable in crowded spaces.

"Are you okay?" Kane asked, jolting her, and she turned to smile up at him.

"Yes, just fine. I, uh, it's just a…" Iris pointed at her head and made a swirling motion with her finger.

"Your guides are talking to you?" Kane gripped her elbow and directed her neatly through the crowd to two seats at the bar next to an old man who Iris instantly recognized as the man from the photo in Aislinn's shop.

"Not my guides. Everyone else's," Iris said. She smiled as Cait skidded to a stop in front of her behind the bar.

"Iris! I've been meaning to come by and talk to you. We've been mad busy after that festival ended a few weeks ago. Everyone seems to have taken an extended holiday. Wine?"

"Sure, great, thanks," Iris said.

"Pint of Guinness?" Cait asked Kane and began to build it before waiting for his answer. It made sense. Even if he didn't want it, someone would likely order a Guinness by the time the pint was finished building.

"Thanks," Kane said with a nod. "You look nice."

"Thanks," Cait and Iris said simultaneously, and Iris laughed when Cait winked at her and bent to grab a bottle of wine. The pub was hopping tonight, and Cait seemed to be doing ten things at once. A glass miraculously appeared before her, and Cait poured her wine.

"This one's on me. To welcome family. Plus, I hear you'll be opening a shop here. We like to support local," Cait said, and Iris's mouth dropped open. Immediately, panic slipped through her.

"How did you…but I haven't…"

"Small town, honey. We're all very excited about it." Cait patted her hand. "You'll get used to everyone knowing your business soon enough."

"Are you the psychic then?" The man next to her smiled. "I heard you're setting up shop next to Beatrice. Lovely woman. She won't give me the time of day, but I still try."

"That's because you're about two decades too old for her, Mr. Murphy," Cait called.

"A man can dream, can't he?" Mr. Murphy shook his head sadly. "Everyone calls me Mr. Murphy. And you are?"

"Iris, and this is Kane," Iris said, pointing to where Kane had remained silent at her side.

"Nice to meet you both. I'm pleased you're taking over the space next to Beatrice. I don't like to think of her being alone in that building. Plus, a psychic shop sounds like a fun job. Do you enjoy it?"

"I...I do," Iris admitted. She took a sip of her wine and let the cool liquid slip down her throat. Right, so the word was out about her business. No going back now. And, if she was reading this correctly, it *seemed* like people would be welcoming.

"Well, sure, and that's all that matters, isn't it? Life goes by so quickly. Why waste it at a job that you don't enjoy?" Mr. Murphy shrugged.

"Every job has parts that aren't great about it," Cait weighed in as she slid Kane's pint to him.

"Naturally, but you just have to find one where the parts you don't like are far outweighed by the parts you do," Mr. Murphy said. "Plus, she'll get to be next to Beatrice all day, which is a big plus in my book."

"And Bubbles," Iris chimed in, amused with them both. "We can't forget Bubbles now."

"Please tell me you're opening that strip club after all?" Kane whispered in her ear, a hopeful note in his voice.

"Bubbles is a cat." Iris turned her head to glare at Kane and found his face still close to her ear. She caught herself wanting to lean forward and nip at his mouth. Instead, she eased back.

"And this is a plus, why?" Kane asked, leaning back on his stool and crossing his arms over his chest.

"Uh-oh, don't let Beatrice hear you say that." Mr. Murphy shook his head and clucked his tongue. "She'll throw you right out."

"Don't tell me you're not a cat person?" Iris stared at Kane. Maybe she'd finally found something not to like about the man.

"Nope, dogs are the superior pet," Kane said.

"Here we go…" Mr. Murphy muttered and signaled to Cait to fill his pint glass.

"No way are dogs the superior pet. Cats are far superior. They're like graceful goddesses that bless your life with their presence," Iris argued.

"Dogs will alert you if there is a fire or an intruder. They'll protect you. Snuggle with you. Make you laugh. Dogs are your best friends. Cats, well, they're annoying." Kane shrugged.

"Annoying! How can an animal be annoying?" Iris gasped.

"They're standoffish. Aloof. They look like these cute fluffballs, but you try to pet them, they grow a thousand teeth and sharp talons. Little puffballs of rage are what they are. Who wants a fluffy rage ball in the house?" Kane demanded.

"Have you lived with a woman before, boyo?" Mr. Murphy piped in and then winced at Iris's glare.

"Cats are easy to care for, excellent companions, and far less messy and cumbersome than dogs," Iris said.

"Yeah, but what's life without messy and cumbersome? As you know, nothing is neat and tidy," Kane said, his eyes hot on hers.

"It's not…it's just…" Iris sputtered. A hand on her shoulder had her turning.

"Iris! I was hoping you'd be here," Gracie said, beaming at her. A man and a woman stood behind her, waiting for introductions. "This is Niamh and Mac. I've been wanting you to meet them."

"Oh, no way." Kane turned and beamed at the man, offering him his hand. "Nice match last week, man. I'm Kane."

"Thanks." Mac grinned at Kane, and Iris remembered he was supposed to be a big deal. Judging by the way the crowd was shifting and whispering, darting looks their way, it seemed to be the truth. He turned to her. "I'm Mac. I think we're cousins of sorts."

"That's what I hear. It's nice to meet you both," Iris said, shaking both of their hands. She wasn't sure what she was supposed to do. Should she hug Mac? Ask him about his family? Invite him over for Christmas? It was such a murky area to her. She wasn't sure how to proceed or what the expectation would be of her.

Niamh looked at Iris and, seeming to understand her dilemma, took charge.

"We're just excited to meet some of Mac's kin. He's got a small family, so even if it's a long-lost second cousin or something of the like, it feels nice to know there's a connection. But we make our own family, don't we, love?" Niamh looked up at Mac, adoration in her eyes, as he pulled her into the crook of his arm.

"That's a relief, I'll admit," Iris said, blowing out a breath. "I only have my mother and never knew my father. There's no other family for me that I'm aware of. I guess I wasn't sure what you expected from me."

"Nothing more than a pint and a chat at the moment," Mac grinned at her and accepted the pint that Cait passed across the bar. "Family is a tricky word for me. I'm still learning how to accept hers into my life."

"Oh, please." Niamh arched a brow at Mac. "You talk to my father more than I do."

"Yeah, about sports. I can't help that the man has a lot of opinions."

"Yesterday, you discussed if you should buy a new car and if he'd come test drive them with you," Niamh pointed out.

"What kind of car are you thinking about?" Kane perked up, and Niamh sighed, rolling her eyes, as the men bent forward to talk about engines.

"I want you to know you're welcome here," Niamh said. She squeezed Iris's arm and held her look. "We're all like you. In our own unique way, of course, and we each have our own...abilities. You'll not be judged here. If you're looking for family, even from those who aren't related to you, this is the place for you."

"I..." Iris was surprised to feel her throat catch. "That's incredibly kind of you. Everyone here has been so nice to me."

"We have to protect our own, don't we? The outside world isn't so kind to those with special abilities, are they?" Niamh furrowed her brow. "I work with kids with abilities like ours. It's...kids can be brutal. But we're not.

You'll come to me if there are any problems? I'm not here full-time, what with Mac's schedule, but I'll give you my number."

"Thank you, Niamh. Honestly? I wasn't expecting this. Any of this," Iris said, swooping her hand out in a circular motion. "It kind of feels like coming home."

"And maybe you are. It sounds like you plan to stay long enough to find out." Niamh turned when Mac pulled her hand, and Iris looked out into the crowded pub, forcing herself to get control of her emotions.

Was it true? Had she finally found home?

A shout went up as music started from a booth up front, and people rushed to pull chairs and tables to the sides. A couple walked out onto the makeshift dance floor and faced off.

"Oh, it's a gonna be a lively one tonight, Cait," Mr. Murphy crowed.

"These two at it again. They're convinced nobody can dance better than them." Cait shook her head.

"They're likely not wrong," Mr. Murphy laughed as the couple began a complicated series of Irish dance steps, their heels sounding sharply against the wood floors, their fists at their waists. Captivated, Iris clapped along and hollered as the music picked up speed and the dancers followed the tune. When the song finished on a resounding high, the dancers ended on the same beat, and the crowd roared in appreciation.

"Come on, Iris, let's see if you can keep up." Kane grabbed her hand and tugged her from her seat.

"No, no, no…" Iris protested, leaning back as he leveraged her forward. "I can't dance like them."

"Give it a go. It's not a true pub experience if you don't try some Irish dancing, is it?" Kane challenged her, and Iris felt her blood heat. She had Irish ancestry, didn't she? Maybe this would come naturally to her. As other couples faced off across the dance floor, Iris tossed her hair and raised her chin.

"Do try to keep up, darling." Kane flashed a wicked smile at her that had her toes curling in her boots.

"Don't darling me. You're the one who..." Iris trailed off as the music started, and Kane launched into a complicated set of steps directly on the beat. That little...annoyance flared, and she followed suit, trying to land on the beat, stomping her heels lightly on the wood floor. Kane laughed, throwing his head back, and picked up the pace. Iris's heart caught as she tried to match his pace, not caring if she looked like a fool, only wanting to try to keep up at this point. Of course the man knew how to Irish dance. She'd yet to see him not be good at anything. When she stumbled, Kane was there, sweeping her into his arms and bouncing across the dance floor. She was light-headed as he dipped her, his lips hovering dangerously close to hers, before righting her once more and twirling her in time to the music. The night took on a hazy quality as the people around her blurred, and all she could feel was Kane spinning, spinning, spinning her. She gave in to it, allowing him to lead, trusting he'd catch her again if she stumbled.

She trusted him, Iris realized, blinking up at his handsome face in awe. Could she trust again that easily? Should she be worried that she did? Confused but caught in the moment, Iris let him lead until he drew her off the dance floor, both gasping for breath. Iris felt like her world had tilted at the revelation, and now she felt nervous and unsure around Kane.

"Another glass of wine?" Kane asked as they returned to the bar, where a crowd clustered around Cait. A leather-bound book was open on the bar, and she wrote rapidly in the book, one finger in the air.

"Two more weeks? Is that a final decision for you, Mr. Murphy?" Cait demanded.

"Sure, and I'm torn, I am. It could be sooner," Mr. Murphy mused.

"You'll need to pick a date then. I'll…" Cait trailed off when she saw Iris and Kane, and she slammed the book closed, neatly putting it beneath the bar. "Kane! Another drink?"

Iris narrowed her eyes at Cait, her bullshit radar going off. What had they been betting on in that book? But before she could ask, Kane turned to her.

"Did you want another drink?"

She did. And she didn't. While tonight had been fun, Iris realized that she was still more than a little over-whelmed by the day's developments. Not only had…something flourished between her and Kane, but she'd also met more of her family and discovered that the whole town knew about her shop. It was too much, and she was approaching sensory overload. It already took a fair amount of work to mute the spirit guides, but muting her own emotions?

"I'm ready to go home. But thank you. I'm tired from all the moving," Iris said.

"No problem, you walk the girl home, Kane. I've got your tab," Cait instructed.

Iris took the time to exchange phone numbers with Niamh and Mac, with the promise of a cup of tea the next day, and soon she was gulping breaths in the cool night air.

"Oh, I needed this. Thank you, Kane. You don't have to walk me home. I'm just down the hill." Iris gestured.

"Get moving, woman. I'm walking you home," Kane said, nudging her, and her body warmed at his touch. They walked in silence for a moment while Iris tried to gather her racing thoughts. Before she knew it, they were at the door to her apartment building, and Iris steeled herself for Kane to ask to come up.

"All good." Kane smiled at her, rocking back on his feet, his hands in his pockets. "Sweet dreams, Iris."

"Oh..." Iris blinked up at him, realizing he was truly just walking her home. Did he not want to come up? Had he changed his mind after their encounter earlier today? Confused, she nibbled her bottom lip as she looked up at him.

"Is it a good night kiss you're wanting?" Kane sighed, pretending to be put upon. "If it's what the lady desires..."

"I didn't say..." His lips cut off her words, the softest brush of a kiss, and Iris sighed. Kane paused, bumping his forehead against hers, and kissed her softly once more.

"Sleep well, sweet Iris. I'll text you tomorrow."

Kane waited as she unlocked the door, fumbling far longer with the key than necessary, then hurtled her way up the stairs.

She was confused, aroused, and overwhelmed. Striding over to her kitchenette, she dug into her cupboard for her emergency stack of chocolate.

If any day called for chocolate, this was one such day.

$\mathcal{T}$he next week passed in a blur for Iris. While she was used to maintaining a busy schedule, this week was far more labor-intensive than anything she'd done recently. She'd drop into bed each night, exhausted, and sleep straight through to the morning.

True to their promise, Niamh and Mac stopped by her store twice before returning to Dublin for Mac's training schedule. Once they'd seen the state of her store and assessed that she had little to no furniture, Mac ordered Iris into his large SUV. The three of them had taken an impromptu road trip and had stopped at several flea markets and vintage stores. Mother Jones was a favorite of Iris's, a funky flea market with stalls featuring vintage and local crafts. Mac had packed his SUV full of the smaller pieces and had arranged to ship the larger items. It had been a bit of a whirlwind, Iris had to admit, but she'd ended up having a lot of fun.

Fun. It was kind of a foreign concept to her, she'd realized about halfway through the next day when she'd been unpacking some of her thrift store finds. Mac and Niamh had been on the other side of the room, arguing over whether her cupboards needed to be painted when Gracie and Dylan had waltzed through the door with a box of pastries and a jug of mimosas. They'd even brought a portable speaker with them, and soon the four of them were arguing over paint colors while Iris had blinked at them, bemused at these people who had somehow woven themselves seamlessly into her life.

It...It made her feel good, she realized, and it stressed her out at the same time. Iris wasn't sure how to operate within this many levels of relationships, friends and family alike, and worry that she would let someone down or not meet expectations gnawed at her. She tried to push it aside and enjoy the moment, but she still hovered in this weird spot between fun and waiting for everything to implode on her.

Just like it had the last time she'd allowed herself to dream.

Iris could kick herself, she thought, and shook her head as she unwrapped some crystals she'd purchased. It still galled her to think that she had been considering buying a home with Warren and settling down. Even the idea of a baby had flitted through her mind occasionally, though it hadn't been the driving force behind Iris daydreaming about getting a house with Warren. No, she'd wanted a home of her own, one where she didn't feel like it could be taken away from her at any moment, and she'd thought that perhaps she could have that future with Warren.

Which showed her just how silly she was to dream.

Iris reminded herself, for the hundredth time that week,

that it was okay to dream. Her anxiety about building something new on her own and forging relationships with new people was a normal response to trauma. She'd been wronged by someone she'd trusted. Even so, Iris refused to let her past stop her from moving forward.

She'd just have to allow herself to be uncomfortable until she got where she needed to go. Wasn't that what growth was about? Discomfort and the unfamiliar?

Speaking of discomfort of another kind, Kane had shown up every day this week. Did her heart leap every time she saw his smiling face at the door? Yes. Did she studiously ignore the fact that she'd fallen apart all over him while having one of the best orgasms of her life on this very dining table? Also, yes. He had not given her any indication that he even remembered the encounter. Iris huffed an annoyed breath as she ripped the tape off another box. For all she could tell, Kane was more than happy to follow her "just friends" initiative.

She only had herself to blame for that one.

> Kane: He's starting to fall for her. He's not good at this whole fake-dating thing. He's never actually been in a real relationship before.

> Iris: So what's the problem?

> Kane: He can't separate reality from fiction. She's following the rules of fake dating, treating him romantically in public when the paparazzi are watching but, back in private, she's put him in the friend zone.

Iris: But they are friends, aren't they? Isn't that what they agreed on?

Kane: Are they friends? She works for the PR company his record label hired. She's just doing her job.

Iris: Fake dating sounds above and beyond her job duties. Why would she agree to that unless she liked him?

Kane: Maybe the PR company gave her a special bonus to stick with him? Since she's the only one he tolerates being close to him?

Iris: Ah, grumpy and a rock star. Be still my heart.

Kane: Do women actually like grumpy men? Why would you want to hang out with someone who is a jerk all the time?

Iris: Women like being the one to make the grumpy guy turn not grumpy. It's one of those fantasy things. Dude's a jerk to everyone and impossible to be around– except with her. It makes her special.

Kane: So if he wants her to fall for him, he needs to make her feel special.

Iris: Well, yeah. Duh. That goes for any relationship, no?

> Kane: Yeah, stupid question. I was just thinking out loud. So she's keeping him at arm's length, and he's falling hard. It scares him, though. Everybody in his life has let him down. He's used for his fame constantly. How can he trust?

Iris's breath caught. Was he still talking about his story? Or were there subliminal messages going on here? She was keeping Kane at arm's length. Or was she? He was the one acting like nothing had happened between them. Maybe he had more feelings there than he was ready to admit. Maybe Iris did too. She had to admit, if only to herself, that she thought about Kane much more than she wanted to. She'd begun to look forward to his texts each day or caught herself staring out the front window, hoping he would stop by to see her again.

> Iris: What happens if he doesn't trust her?

Kane: Hmm, good question. Let's see... he'll fall back into an endless routine of rock stardom where nothing has meaning because it is a revolving door of women and groupies, where nobody actually cares about him. He'll have to decide if he loses the record label to his father by refusing his grandfather's edict to marry an arranged bride, or if the loss would be worth it to have this girl by his side. He's never not had the comfort of the record label supporting him, so turning his back on that and giving his father the controlling stake could be catastrophic for him as a person. But so could losing her.

Iris: Big decisions. What happens if he does trust her and tells her about his feelings for her in an open and honest manner? Like an adult?

Kane: Well, for one, that doesn't make for good television.

Iris: I suppose not. Where's the drama of it all?

Kane: Exactly. But if he does trust her with his feelings, which he'd be doing for the first time ever with a woman, she could do one of two things.

Iris: Murder him?

Kane: Right, one of three things, I suppose. There's always murder, though it would be a very unsuspecting plot twist in a rom-com, you bloodthirsty woman. Either she rejects him, like everyone else in his life, and he falls apart. Or she returns his feelings and...

Iris: And?

Kane: She rescues him. Nothing matters about how the future unfolds so long as they are together.

Iris: Sigh, my heart.

Kane: Okay, I'm good here. See you later.

Iris grinned down at the phone, loving how casually he expected to stop by and see her. He'd stopped asking if he could meet up with her, instead just showing up each day and making himself indispensable.

The shop was coming along nicely, as was her apartment upstairs. Both still needed a lot of work, and Iris wasn't going to rush it. But the design for both was beginning to take shape, and Iris could see her vision coming to life.

Her vision.

Not Warren's, not anyone else's. Sure, her friends here had weighed in and argued about decorating choices, but they'd always defaulted to Iris to make the final decision. Knowing that people respected her choices felt good, and she hummed as she divided her crystals into small bowls. On a whim, Iris decided to make her shop more than just a place for her to conduct her readings. She'd decided to also sell a few things for those who were more magickly inclined. She thought she could do private readings three days a week and open her shop for the other two. That way, she'd have a nice balance between the emotional drain that came with reading clients and the excitement of meeting new people and selling items in her shop. She'd already booked Gracie's line of products, some of Aislinn's and Kira's prints, and had arranged for a bulk supplier for her crystals.

When the bells over the door sounded an hour later, Iris smiled as Kane buzzed into the shop.

"I've got my painting clothes on, and I'm ready to tackle that wall," Kane said as a way of hello. Iris's heart sighed. The man wore gray sweatpants and a fitted T-shirt. Did men have any idea how good they looked in gray sweats? It was a dangerous combination, that sexy mixed with cuddly. She dragged her eyes away from him before she did something stupid like crawl on his lap.

"You don't have to do that. I'm capable of painting, you know," Iris said, rolling her eyes at him.

"I know, but you're busy. Look at all those boxes you still have to unpack," Kane said. He breezed past her, absentmindedly pressing a kiss to her cheek, before moving to where she'd piled painting supplies on the floor. He smelled like soap and bad decisions, and Iris had to actively clench her fists to stop herself from crossing to him and wrapping her arms around his waist. It had to be a crime to look that good in sweatpants. Iris deliberately turned away as Kane cracked the lid on the paint can.

"Oh, good color," Kane said.

"Thanks, I loved the moody blue," Iris agreed. She'd

picked a deep, almost midnight blue color that boasted soft turquoise undertones. It contrasted nicely with the honey wood floors and the beams that crossed the ceiling. Iris could just see her painting from Aislinn's store on the wall here, and she looked forward to hanging it in her store. She had already decided that would be the finishing touch, as it would mean she was finally home.

"I do too. It will showcase your artwork nicely and just adds a punch to this room. You shouldn't be afraid to go bold, you know? I bet, with some of those rugs you picked out and that cool vintage furniture, it will make your clients really comfortable when they come in for a reading."

As Kane chattered about her clients and what they'd like about her shop, dread grew in Iris's stomach. He was just so...there. Involved. As though he ran the business with her.

No, this was not what she wanted.

Iris wanted to do this on her own. She needed to do it on her own. This was her shop, not hers and Kane's. She slammed a box down on the table, panic gripping her, as she tried to methodically unpack the boxes of tarot cards she'd ordered.

She was being stupid. It wasn't like Kane had invested in her business.

But neither had Warren.

It had started just like this.

As the realization dawned, Iris dropped the box of tarot cards she was holding and gaped at Kane. Her dependency on Warren had started just like this. He'd come in, helped her pick her shop and, soon, he'd been decorating it with her as well, though, admittedly, he'd been far more controlling of the pieces she'd picked. Still, he'd been there from day one. Making himself indispensable.

Up to the point when he'd destroyed her.

Her breath came in shallow pants, and she gripped the table's edges, trying to force the panic down. She was so stupid to think she was changing her path and growing. Instead, she'd waltzed right into the same pattern she'd been in before. Talk about a comfort blanket and all that…

"Iris. What's wrong?" Kane replaced the lid on the paint and crossed to her. When he reached for her, she put a hand in the air.

"I can't. This…I can't…it's too. You're too…" Iris waved her hands in the air, gulping for breath.

"I'm what?" Kane asked, confusion on his face.

"You're here. You're too here. Involved. Nice. I'm supposed to do this on my own." Iris gasped, fanning her face. She couldn't bring herself to look at him, feeling like she was kicking a puppy.

"Just breathe," Kane said, keeping his voice calm.

Iris gripped the table again and bent over, sucking her breath in. She started when he lifted her hair, then released a sigh when a cool cloth touched the sensitive skin at the back of her neck.

"Thanks," Iris bit out.

"That usually helps me. I don't have ice, but ice helps, too, when my anxiety gets too bad. Just dunking your face in a bowl of ice water can sometimes stop a panic attack in its tracks," Kane said.

"Duly noted," Iris said. She needed him to leave. He was too close.

She was too close.

To falling for this man.

"You know what you need?" Kane asked.

"What's that?" Iris asked and, despite wanting space from him, curiosity won out.

"Otters," Kane said.

"Otters?" At that, Iris did look up, confusion pushing her anxiety aside.

"Yup. Otters. In the car, Iris. You're going for a ride."

"No, I can't. I have things to do. That's the point…I can't just follow what you want…" Iris stopped when Kane held up his hand.

"The otters are hungry, Iris. Are you saying they don't deserve food too?"

"What does that even have to do with anything? I have so much work to do. Here. Not at an otter farm. Or whatever…" Iris said.

"Precisely the point. Get your coat." Kane stood at the door, keys in hand, and Iris knew he wouldn't take no for an answer.

"What if I hate otters?" Iris grumbled, mad at him for no reason and every reason.

"Then we'll just have to change your opinion, won't we?" Kane grinned at Iris when she bared her teeth at him, but his ploy worked, and her panic attack receded.

Just another reason to be annoyed with him.

CHAPTER 17

*T*he panic was easy to recognize.

It was the same that he'd seen in his own reflection over the past six months of being unable to write. The ice trick was something Grant had told him about and, he had to admit, there was a time or two that it had come through for him. He hated seeing the same look in Iris's eyes, as though she was a cornered animal ready to lash out, but he also could understand where her emotions came from.

In many respects, she was fighting for her life.

It didn't take a psychology degree to make the leap that Kane's presence in Iris's life was triggering for her at the moment. Particularly when she was so fresh from a catastrophic breakup that had destroyed her business. It wasn't like this was some nine-to-five job where she clocked in, took a paycheck, and never thought about work at home. For Iris, work was deeply personal.

Kane could understand that. His was much the same. So personal, in fact, that he'd yet to disclose his pen name to Iris. A few times, he had toyed with telling her that he wrote the books she had raved about, but then he'd stopped. He wanted Iris to like him for him, not for his fame. Maybe it wasn't the best move, but he would tell her eventually. Knowing her and her abilities, she probably already knew who he was and was just respecting his privacy.

Which, again, made him like her even more.

"Did you know that otters often hook paws when they sleep so they don't drift away from each other?" Kane asked, following the winding road that led them away from the village and toward the cove. Iris eyed him owlishly.

"Why do you even know that?"

"I have no idea. It's just one of those random facts that I picked up along the way somewhere." Kane laughed, nudging the volume up on the radio as the Rolling Stones complained about their lack of satisfaction.

"Kane. Why are we going to see otters?" Iris asked.

"Because you need some time away from your shop and to get out of your head. What better way to do that than in nature? Plus, otters are cute. Have you seen any before?"

"I live in Boston. I see rats," Iris mumbled. Her fingers tapped an uneven rhythm on her leg.

"Then you're in for a treat. You can't be stressed out around otters," Kane said.

"Why? Will they attack?" Iris asked, causing Kane to laugh.

"Yes, these are murderous otters. They sense any stress and feed on your rage. You'd better remain calm around them, or they'll call their army to attack."

"I think you're kidding, but I can't be sure. I'll just keep my distance from rage otters," Iris mumbled.

Kane chuckled and turned the music up more, giving Iris time to collect herself on the drive. He knew that a near-miss with a panic attack would often leave him drained or emotionally raw. If she had some time to breathe and see that she was safe here, hopefully, she'd feel better soon.

Kane drove past Gracie's cottage, waving at Rosie, who raced across the fields and higher up into the hills. There, they came upon a sign for a nature center and a sign directing them to the otter pond. Kane turned to the otter pond, suspecting that Iris wasn't in the mood to visit any exhibitions at the moment. He hummed along to the music as they trundled their way up the dirt road until they finally reached a small gravel car park. Kane pulled the car to a stop and shut off the engine before turning to Iris.

"Ready?"

"I suppose." Iris shrugged. Some color had returned to her cheeks, which Kane considered to be a good sign, and he got out of the car. She was already out before he could hold the door for her. She shoved her hands in her coat pockets and looked cautiously around at the empty green fields that sloped gently down to where the cliffs met the water. A light gust of wind tickled his cheeks, bringing with it the scent of saltwater.

"Come on, let's go find these little beasts," Kane said. He wrapped an arm around Iris's shoulder, pulling her close, and was surprised she allowed it. She really must be shaken or scared of the otters. Either way, he would appreciate this time with her cuddling into his side.

It had taken all of his willpower to continue to treat her lightly over this past week since he'd almost devoured her on the table at her shop. The image of her, skin flushed, luscious pink breasts bobbing in the air while she'd collapsed around him, well, it had fueled many a late-night dream for Kane. He thought about her constantly and was dying for another taste of her lips. Yet Kane sensed that if he moved too fast, Iris would just push him away. Today was a perfect example of that. He understood he had his work cut out for him if he wanted to convince Iris to take a chance on him.

And he did.

He really, really did. Not only did Kane want her in his bed, but he wanted her in his life. Watching her move fearlessly forward in the wake of her life falling apart had only fueled his courage to do the same. He admired her pluck and how she took risks and figured out the answers later.

She was slowly rescuing him, even if she didn't realize it.

"There, see? That's a nice spot to have a sit, isn't it then?" Kane pointed at a bench set on the edge of a small pond, and Iris murmured her agreement. Directing her to the bench, he pulled her down next to him and kept his arm around her shoulders to see if she would allow the cuddle. When she did, he looked down and saw her staring morosely at the water.

"I don't see any otters," Iris said.

"No, I don't either. But we've only just arrived. Let's sit a while, shall we?"

"And do what?" Iris poked her lower lip out in a pout.

"Talk?" Kane suggested. "Why don't you tell me what's got you all worked up?"

"Mmmm." Iris made a noncommittal noise and shrugged a shoulder.

"Would you like me to take a stab at this?"

"You're not going to let it go, are you?" Iris pulled back, nudging his arm off her shoulders, and glared at him. "Do we have to make this a huge thing? I just had some anxiety, okay? It happens."

Kane watched as she tilted her head and shook it, muttering to herself, and he wondered what her spirit guides were saying to her.

"Normally, yes, I'd let these things go. But I think there's something deeper there, and since I suspect it involves me, well, no, I'll not be letting it go, then."

"You're annoying," Iris said, a mutinous look on her face.

"Yeah, but I'm cute. So I can get away with it." Kane bumped her shoulder with his, and she made a noise that sounded suspiciously like a growl. "I'm guessing you're drawing some parallels between your ex running your business with you and me coming around to help?"

"Something like that." Iris bit the words out.

"And you're worried that you're just making the same mistakes all over again? Falling into the same patterns."

"Yup, that about sums it up."

"You're not wrong to feel this way," Kane said, and Iris glanced at him, surprise written on that pretty mismatched face of hers. "It makes absolute sense. Plus, our brains naturally look for patterns, so it's easy to see why you'd lump me in with your ex-boyfriend, insulting though it is."

"I'm not trying to insult you. These are just my feelings." Iris hunched her shoulders, and Kane ached to hold her once more and promise her that everything would work out just fine.

"And I'm telling you they are valid," Kane said. He turned to look out over the water as he formulated his thoughts. "I don't mind you being scared or anxious that my help with your business is similar to how Warren involved himself in your previous shop. However, if you're going to look for similarities, then it's only fair you look for differences too. Have I signed any contracts with you?"

"You have not," Iris whispered.

"Have I, at any point, told you what to do? What color to paint? What furniture to buy? What logo to design? What toilet paper to buy?"

At that, Iris cracked a smile.

"You have not."

"Have I asked for account information, passwords, keys, or any other private or security-related information?"

"You have not."

"Have I asked if I can help you run the business or become involved with your social media following?"

"You have not." Iris sighed.

"What have I done, then?" Kane wanted her to say it, so she could really understand for herself how he was worlds apart from that jerk of an ex-boyfriend who had ridden her coattails to success.

"You've shown up every day, often with snacks. Then you ask me what I need. And then…"

"I do it." Kane raised his eyebrows at her.

"You do," Iris agreed. She sighed and pinched her nose. "I'm sorry. I'm sorry. I'm sorry. You're entirely right. Just because you're male and I'm attracted to you doesn't mean that you're anything like Warren. That wasn't fair of me to lump you in with him."

"You're attracted to me?" Kane perked up. "Tell me how. And in full details."

"Oh, right, like I'm going to feed that ego of yours." Iris shot him a look.

"Ego? Hardly," Kane scoffed.

"Well, I suppose that's fair. You're confident, but I wouldn't say you have a big ego. But I've met you at a difficult time in your life."

Kane reached over and picked up Iris's hand, threading his fingers through hers.

"You may not know it, Iris, but you're rescuing me."

"What? I am?" Iris said, turning to Kane.

"You are. I…I so admire you. You, who had your world shattered at your feet, picked yourself up the next damn day and hopped on a plane to another country. You've met new family, started a new business, and even found a new place to live. It's pretty incredible to watch. You've inspired me to work on moving past my own hurts and to make progress in my own life."

"Kane." Iris's voice caught, and a sheen of tears shimmered in her eyes.

"I didn't bring you up here to make you cry again," Kane said, reaching over to run a finger over her lips. "But

I'd be remiss in my role of knight in shining armor if I didn't tell you how much you've helped me."

"Why do you have to go and get hotter every time I talk to you?" Iris glared, and Kane threw his head back and laughed.

"Well, now, I think we should unpack that a little bit more, don't you? Like…the fact I've been dying to kiss you for days now. Do you want another kiss from me, Iris? Have you thought about my touch as well?" Kane found his answer when her cheeks flushed, and she bit her lower lip.

"You didn't come up." Iris surprised him just as he leaned down to kiss her.

"I didn't come…you mean after the pub? Last week?" Kane asked. Score one for strategy on his part, he thought. Pleased that it had bothered her that he'd left her with just a kiss, Kane bit back a smile. He wasn't playing games with her, not necessarily, but he already knew that a dance with Iris would be one step forward and two steps back. He didn't want to screw this up.

"Yes. You just…went home."

"You didn't invite me up," Kane reminded her.

"Maybe you didn't want to." Iris shrugged a shoulder, glaring out at the surface of the pond.

"Oh, now that impression I'm happy to correct. You see, I very much wanted to." Kane leaned over, nipped at her earlobe, and then pressed a kiss to the sensitive skin at the nape of her neck. "I wanted to do many delightfully naughty things to you. I still do. But I was following your request if you recall?"

"What…what request was that?" Iris turned, her lips an

inch from his, her eyes huge in her face. The moment drew out, energy pulsing between them, and lust pooled low in Kane's gut.

"You told me...only a little. Remember? When I had you sprawled out before me, aching with need, riding me?"

"Kane!" Iris gasped, but he could tell she was turned on just thinking about their moment together.

"You asked for just a little. And I've respected that. I respect you, Iris. I'm always going to let you lead." Kane closed the gap between them. "Until I'm not." Then his lips were on hers, and she moaned, surprising him when she bit his lip lightly and then sucked gently, making his entire body alert. He wanted nothing more than to pick her up off this bench and lay her down in the soft grass by the pond, slowly exploring her body until she came undone for him once more.

A splash sounded behind them, and Iris pulled away, her lips slick, her eyes heavy with lust.

"Look!" Iris exclaimed, gripping his arm. Kane pulled her into him, cuddling her close, trying to tamp down his need for her before turning his head.

There, a family of otters had appeared from wherever their den was. There looked to be an older couple and several young pups. The pups zipped around the pond's surface, frolicking in the water, diving beneath the surface and popping up several feet later. They were cute, fluffy, and an absolute buzzkill for his seduction of Iris. But when she laughed for the first time that day, delighted with the otter antics, Kane let it go. There would be another time and place for him to show Iris just how much he cared for her.

For now, it was just enough to see her eyes light and hear her laughter trill across the wind. At the very least, he'd done his job as a friend and as a lover.

Iris was steady on her feet again, and that was all that mattered to him.

CHAPTER 18

"*I* should be your first customer."

Iris looked up as Beatrice strode into her shop, which was not yet open to the public, and slapped some money on the counter.

"Um, sure, I can do that. If you'd like to book an…" Iris trailed off as Bubbles followed Beatrice in, and the old woman returned to the front door to ensure it was closed.

"No, right now," Beatrice said, plopping down in one of the armchairs Iris had found at a vintage shop. The material was soft velvet, and the print was faded dusty roses on a turquoise backdrop. She'd immediately fallen in love with them, and Mac had graciously moved them for her. She was coming to enjoy the idea of having a cousin, particularly one like Mac. He was cheerful, super strong, and exceedingly helpful. They'd easily bonded over feeling at odds as kids growing up, and Iris looked forward to the next time he'd swing through town.

More and more people were stopping by daily to introduce themselves. In fact, it was a wonder Iris was getting anything done, what with the number of villagers who dropped by to meet her and inquire about her services. Some people did so with barely concealed judgment, which Iris was well used to by now, but most were open and friendly, and Iris was starting to feel like she was actually becoming a part of a lovely little community.

"I don't usually perform on demand, Beatrice. I'm not at anyone's beck and call." Iris infused a gentle note into her tone so Beatrice knew she was educating her and not trying to be rude.

"Oh right. I suppose that was rude of me, wasn't it? I've been trying to bide my time, but I'm just too excited." Beatrice all but bounced in her shoes. Iris regarded the old woman who wore a sunny-yellow cardigan and neon-pink sneakers. She'd been nothing but kind and helpful to Iris, and they'd developed an affectionate friendship over the past few weeks. It wouldn't hurt for Iris to give her a reading.

"Fair enough. Why don't we settle in, and I'll just see what comes up? We'll call it an informal reading unless you have any pressing questions you'd like answered at the moment?"

"No, none that I can think of. Unless there's anything I need to know for Bubbles's welfare?" Beatrice looked down at where Bubbles had wound herself between Iris's feet.

"I'm not really an animal communicator, but if anything pops up for me, I'll let you know." Iris smiled and held her hands in the air. She began with a short invocation, inviting the spirit guides in and asking for protection of their space while they worked together. Closing her eyes, Iris waited while Ophelia and Lara chattered at her. They were always delighted when Iris did a reading because they also met new spirit guides. It was kind of like they were all having a little party up there. Finally, Ophelia came forward with a male spirit guide.

"This is Jacob. He was Beatrice's husband in this lifetime." Ophelia made introductions, and Iris's lips curved. Beatrice had spoken fondly of her husband, who had passed from a sudden heart attack a few years back. They'd been high school sweethearts and had enjoyed many years together.

"Jacob is here," Iris said.

"You don't say!" Beatrice exclaimed, slapping her palms on her thighs. "Oh, tell him I love him and miss him."

"I know," Jacob said to Iris, a smile on his face for Beatrice. "Can you tell her what joy she brought to my life? And that I'm honored she chose me to be her partner. Her soul is pure, and I was lucky to have her grace by my side."

Iris relayed the message, and tears sprang to Beatrice's eyes.

"Oh, he'd always go on like that. He was a good man, my Jacob."

"Ask her why she hasn't gone to the safe deposit box yet," Jacob asked.

"Why haven't you gone to open the safe deposit box?" Iris asked, bending over to pet Bubbles, who bumped her head against Iris's leg.

"Oh, he knows that, does he? I…I can't find the key," Beatrice admitted, wringing her hands.

"*It fell behind the desk. It's under the rug,*" Jacob instructed.

Iris relayed the information, and Beatrice brightened.

"Really? I've been looking for that damn thing for years," Beatrice admitted.

"*It has what she needs in there. The deed to the house. Extra cash. Special jewelry. She won't want for anything,*" Jacob instructed.

"He always did look out for me." Beatrice sighed. "Oh, can you tell him I still talk to him? Every morning, I talk to him over my tea. I always wondered if he heard me."

"*I do,*" Jacob said, a smile on his face. "*I'm always there.*"

"Is there a way you can let her know?" Iris asked. Oftentimes, spirit guides would identify a certain sign for their loved ones to look for.

"Let me know what?" Beatrice demanded, but Iris held up her hand while she listened.

"*I'll send her a sparrow. Right on the windowsill by the kitchen table. I'll even see if I can get him to tap three times on the window, but we'll see,*" Jacob said.

"He's going to send you a sparrow when you talk to him in the mornings. It will tap three times on the window if you're lucky."

"Oh! I'd love that," Beatrice exclaimed, her face wreathed in smiles.

"Can you see if Bubbles needs anything?" Iris asked. It was worth a shot.

"*That cat is fit and fine as can be. Though she wants to spend more time in the bookshop. She promises not to run outside if Beatrice allows her to be downstairs with her.*"

Iris relayed the message, and Beatrice eyed Bubbles warily.

"I'm just so scared of losing her," Beatrice said. "She's my only companion now."

"No, she's not. I'm right here. I'm always here," Jacob whispered before fading away. That was usually the way of it. Spirit guides could only come through for so long before they used up much of their energy. Well, other people's spirit guides. Hers seemed like they had enough energy to run several marathons.

"Jacob wanted you to know that you don't just have Bubbles. He says he's always here with you."

"Oh, well, now you've gone and done it." Beatrice fanned her face and then jumped up to give Iris a big hug. "Come on, Bubbles, let's go to the bookstore. We'll see how you do when I open later, okay?" With that, Beatrice disappeared with an armful of cat, tears still streaming down her face, and Iris sighed. Leaning back, she closed her eyes, muttered her closing incantation to round out the session, and took a few breaths to center herself. It wasn't easy dealing with the depth of emotions that came with people wanting to speak to their loved ones who had passed on, though she had grown stronger through the years for it.

"You made her day."

A voice startled Iris's eyes open, and she stared at a woman standing in front of her. But not a woman. An apparition.

"Where did you come from?" Iris narrowed her eyes.

"My name is Fiona. I'm family to Gracie and still

watch over…well, Gracie says I meddle, as much as I'm able to."

"The matriarch," Iris said. She'd already heard about Fiona, but not that the woman still visited in spirit form.

"I suppose, yes, though there were others that came before me," Fiona beamed. "I want you to know I'm proud of you and what you're building here. If you have any doubts, you shouldn't. You'll thrive beautifully in this space. But…I don't have time for more. I'm here to warn you."

"Warn me?" Iris straightened.

"He's coming. Protect yourself." With that, Fiona winked from sight. Taking the ghost at her word, Iris jumped up from her chair and whirled, looking for a weapon. Her heart hammered in her chest, and the door opened just as her hand closed around the handle of a broom. She knew, before she even turned, who stood behind her. Cursing herself for not making sure the door was locked after Beatrice had left, Iris turned slowly.

"It's cute that you think you can just up and start over without me. You'll never be a success." Warren sniffed. Iris studied him, noting he looked the worse for wear and gripped the broom tightly in her hands. Should she scream for Beatrice? However, noting the maniacal light in Warren's eyes, Iris decided against it. She didn't want to put her friend in any danger.

"I'll be just fine without you," Iris clarified, shifting her weight from foot to foot like a boxer, and waited for Warren's next move. "What are you doing here, Warren? How can you travel internationally? Isn't there a warrant out for your arrest?"

"I was already out of the country long before you called the cops on me," Warren made a tsking noise with his mouth, slowly walking forward. Iris stepped back behind the dining table. "You shouldn't have done that, you know. It's your word against mine. And nobody's going to believe a scam artist like yourself."

"I'm not a scam artist. It's you who is the liar," Iris bit out, keeping her eyes on Warren. He'd stopped moving, turning to look at her shop.

"I don't lie. I just…massage the truth a bit. Isn't that what sales is about? You're just selling a dream to some-body. It's not hard to tell people what they want to hear. Don't tell me you didn't do the same. I heard your read-ings. It's all the same, over and over. You're loved. You're missed. It's such bullshit." Warren's laugh cracked. "You should have just let me be, Iris. Now you've got people coming after me? Digging into my accounts. I want my money back."

"Excuse me?" Iris's voice rose a notch. "*You* took *my* money. I want my money back. Have you gone completely off your rocker?"

"Not as of yesterday. My accounts have been emptied. And thank god I still track your location on your iPhone. You weren't hard to find. So give it back, and we'll call it even." Warren advanced, rounding the table.

"I didn't take it! I have no idea who has your, actually, *my* money. Probably the police. If you weren't such a dick, maybe you wouldn't be in this position," Iris seethed. His hand was out, and she was too mad to stop the first blow, his palm cracking sharply across her cheek. She stumbled back, the pain ratcheting up her face, making her senses sharpen. No longer did she care about the money. This was about survival.

Tightening her hands on the broom, she angled it in front of her and backed up just as Warren launched. Grabbing her shoulders, he pinned her to the table, and she brought her knee up between his legs, just missing him as he twisted.

"Stupid bitch. I stayed with your ugly ass way too long. I never should have…"

Iris gasped as suddenly…he was just gone. It was as though someone had lifted him straight into the air, and she blinked in surprise as Warren flew through the air and smacked against the brick wall, landing in an awkward pile of splayed limbs. Iris gaped at Kane, who advanced and lifted Warren as though he weighed nothing. Once the man was back on his feet, Kane made quick work of him, landing punch after punch in the man's face until blood splattered onto the freshly cleaned wood floors.

Realizing that Kane was in a blind rage, as he continued to pummel Warren, Iris jumped up and raced forward, wrapping her arms around Kane's waist from behind.

"I'm safe. I'm safe. I'm safe," Iris shouted over and over, trying to break through to Kane. Finally, as though her words just registered, Kane dropped his arms, and his shoulders slumped. His breath came in heavy pants, and Iris dared to peek around him to see Warren slumped on the floor, mumbling into his palms. Outside, police sirens wailed.

"Did he…" Kane bit out, refusing to look at her, and Iris realized just how on edge he still was.

"Kane...I'm okay. Look at me," Iris whispered, coming to stand in front of him. She dared to reach up and touch his face, bringing his gaze to hers. His eyes heated.

"He hit you," Kane said and made to move forward.

"No, no, you've done enough. I'm safe. Do you hear me? Tell me you hear me," Iris begged, grabbing his arms to stop him from doing more destruction. Warren wasn't worth it, of that much Iris was sure.

"I hear you," Kane said, finally seeming to collapse in on himself. Iris wrapped her arms around him, and he brought his forehead to hers.

"I can't...I just...lost it. He had his hands on you," Kane murmured. "He hurt you. I can't let people hurt you."

"I'm okay. I promise you that I'm okay," Iris whispered. "Thank you for saving me. I was scared, but you helped, okay? You saved me. I'm safe now."

"Thank god," Kane said.

"Well, now, that explains why Bubbles was acting up," Beatrice said from the door, and Iris leaned around Kane to look at her. Bubbles darted inside the room and immediately came to Iris, stretching up to paw at her thigh. Iris scooped the cat up, surprised she was letting her hold her. "The Gardai are here."

"You called the police?" Iris asked, her eyes widening as two men in uniform entered the store.

"Of course. Bubbles was having an absolute fit. I knew something had to be wrong. Better safe than sorry, no?" Beatrice sniffed at the crumbled man on the floor. "You made good work of him, Kane. I'm proud of you."

"What's going on?" Gracie's voice sounded from the

door, and Iris winced. It looked like they were about to have a party.

"Ma'am, we need you to answer some questions." One of the officers approached her and introduced himself.

"His name is Warren Smith. He has a warrant out for his arrest in Boston, and he just assaulted me. Kane came in the door as I was being assaulted and pulled him off me."

"Thank you. We'll get him cuffed and taken in. We'd like to take a formal statement as soon as possible?" the officer asked as his partner spoke quietly to Warren and pulled out handcuffs.

"Of course. I'll follow you right in."

"Are you hurt?" Gracie threw her arms around Iris, cat and all, and Bubbles meowed in annoyance. Dylan loomed behind her, concern on his handsome face.

"He hit me, but I'm okay. Kane saved me," Iris said, her eyes once more going to Kane's face. The man had shut down, seeming to go inside himself, and she wondered if he was upset with her for having to protect her. He'd probably really hurt his hands now that she thought about it, which meant he wouldn't be able to type. Guilt filled her. "Kane, we should get some ice on your hands."

"It's fine," Kane said, barely glancing at his bloody knuckles. Iris looked at Gracie, who just shrugged her shoulders.

"I've got a lovely healing salve that will fix that right up. Come with me," Gracie said. She tugged Kane with her, refusing to take no for an answer, and Kane went to the back of the shop where she'd dropped off a box of her creams to stock Iris's shelves.

"I should have seen this coming," Dylan said, keeping his voice low so the Gardai wouldn't overhear. "I'm so sorry that I didn't. It was hard to pin down his location."

"It was you then?" Iris asked.

"Yes, I figured you'd want your money back. Plus, it's a lot harder to be on the run if your bank account is empty. But I should have thought about the potential repercussions. I didn't think he'd be able to track you," Dylan said. "I'm so sorry."

"No, this is probably better. Truly. Not only will he be charged but maybe he'll learn a lesson or two along the way. I don't think Warren will bother me again."

They watched as the Gardai hauled Warren up from the floor and dragged him from the shop, his head hanging.

"Well, I think this calls for a bit of whiskey. Shall I?" Beatrice clapped her hands.

"Yes, please," Dylan said, and Bubbles hopped out of Iris's arms and followed Beatrice back to the bookstore.

"There now, you're all sorted," Gracie said to Kane when Iris walked to the back of the shop. Iris gaped at his hands, which had just sported raw wounds, and now showed no sign of injury. Kane's face held a bewildered look.

"Those are some creams," Iris said lightly.

"Come on man, let's get that whiskey. You'll get used to the way of things here soon enough," Dylan said, clapping a hand on Kane's shoulder.

CHAPTER 19

*I*ris would have gone to Kane sooner, but by the time she finished with the police in Ireland and the United States, she had a headache the size of Texas. All she wanted to do was crawl into bed, pull a pillow over her head, and mope.

And so, she did just that.

It felt nice, for once, to take care of herself and put her needs first. She was so used to having a full schedule or always answering Warren's demands that she couldn't remember the last time she'd shut the world out for a day. Turned out, it was exactly what she needed. When she woke, groggy and disoriented to a knock on her door hours later, Iris had to wipe the drool from her chin before opening the door to find Beatrice, holding a tray of food, with Bubbles at her feet.

"I shooed everyone away, figuring you needed a rest after your tough day, but I'd at least feel better if you ate something," Beatrice said.

"Everyone?" Iris blinked at her in confusion.

"Oh, sure, and you don't think the whole town doesn't already know what happened?" Beatrice nodded to the hallway, and Iris gaped at where vases of flowers, tins of baked goods, and even one smiley-face balloon sat.

"Are those for me?" Iris stared at the gifts.

"They are. Do you mind if I put this down?" Beatrice pushed past Iris and put the tray on the kitchen counter. There wasn't much in the way of decoration yet, as Iris had been concentrating on her shop, but she had managed to get a new bed and wrangle a small dining set into the space.

"Who are these all from?" Iris asked, bending to pick up several of the vases.

"Let's see. The food is from Cait, who says to call if you want anything else, and she'll have it delivered. Flowers from Gracie, Aislinn, and Kira. Balloon and whiskey from Mac and Niamh. Cookies from Mr. Murphy. A few from the neighboring shops. I made a list for you so you'd know."

"I…" Iris blinked at the tears that rose to her eyes and dropped into a chair at the table. "I don't even know what to say." She felt raw and exposed, like she was standing at the window naked, and everyone was looking at her.

"You say thank you." Beatrice patted her hand. "We look after each other here, Iris. You'll get used to it soon enough."

"But I don't even *know* some of these people," Iris said with a small laugh. "There's no reason for them to bring me baked goods because my ex-boyfriend is awful."

"Sure there is," Beatrice said, her tone sharp enough that Iris looked up. "They do it because you need to believe in the goodness of people. You need to understand community. Family. Just like you'd do the same if someone else was having a hard time."

"Would I?" Iris wondered.

"Of course you would. Now, eat this soup, or Cait's going to ban me from the pub, and how will I let Mr. Murphy flirt with me if I can't go to the pub?"

"Isn't he too old for you?"

"Sure he is. But it makes me feel good, and Jacob wouldn't mind. It's a win-win," Beatrice laughed, and Iris spooned up some of the vegetable stew. Her mind felt soggy, like a saturated sponge, and she didn't quite know what to do with all her feelings that knotted in her stom-ach. "You know what I would do if I were you?"

"What?" Iris looked up at Beatrice.

"I'd take that tin of cookies to Kane's place and thank him properly. Yes, that's certainly what I would do."

"I doubt he wants to see me. I put him in a bad position today. He could have really hurt himself," Iris said. She shrugged a shoulder and scooped up more soup. "Plus, who wants to deal with my mess?"

"Oh, well now, I hadn't thought you were stupid," Beatrice said, causing Iris to choke on the mouthful of soup she'd just taken.

"Excuse me?" Iris wiped her mouth with a napkin. Beatrice had even put a single flower in a tiny vase on the tray. Details, Iris thought. They mattered.

"Truly, you had struck me as a smart woman, but I may have to revise my opinion," Beatrice sniffed and stood. "Let me tell you something, Iris, about a man in love. He'd rather die than see the woman he loves get hurt. Men love differently than women do, you know. You're it for Kane, and the last thing you have to do is feel bad about him having to defend you today. He's likely thrilled that he was there at the right time. You need to thank him and show him that you feel the same way."

"*Love*...Beatrice, surely you're misconstruing things. We're just friends. He was protecting a friend," Iris insisted. Liar, liar, her heart whispered.

"Nope. No, he was *not*. I saw his face and the way he looked at you. That man is a goner. It's on you to accept it or not. Be careful with his feelings, Iris. I like the lad. He's got a good heart."

With that, Beatrice disappeared with Bubbles strolling nonchalantly behind her, and Iris blinked down at her bowl of soup, adding one more layer to the complicated mess of emotions in her stomach. Sighing, she unmuted her spirit guides.

"What should I do?"

"Go to him!" Lara and Ophelia screamed so loudly in her head that Iris immediately put them back on mute. Right, fine, maybe they all had a point. But first, she needed a shower and to make herself presentable. After her shower, she stood in a towel at the mirror and assessed the damage. Warren had managed to crack her right across the cheekbone, and bruising was already starting to show. Iris suspected it would look worse tomorrow, as bruises often did. She nudged the tender skin with her fingers, debating whether to cover it up with makeup, but some of the skin was raw. It wasn't like Kane didn't know what had happened to her. Best to just pat some of Gracie's healing salve on the area and let it be.

However, vanity still won out. Dark circles tinged the delicate skin below her eyes, and Iris realized she looked about as raw as she felt inside. Maybe one of the reasons she struggled so hard to process her own emotions was because she'd spent her whole life absorbing and managing other people's feelings. Somewhere along the way, she'd gotten so good at helping others that she'd forgotten to learn how to help herself. Now, when her thoughts were bouncing around her brain like someone had taken a bat to a wasp nest, she didn't quite know what to do with all the feelings that rose to the surface. It was confusing, this mix of shame and sadness that came with a side of...dare she say happiness? Was it fair or even right that she could feel a sense of lightness after she'd been victimized? Because that's what it was, Iris realized, gripping the side of the sink and taking deep breaths as she spoke some hard truths to herself in the mirror.

Warren had abused her.

While he'd never lifted a hand to her in their relationship, he'd taken advantage of her in a million other ways. Death by a thousand cuts and all that...

It was true, though. He'd worked hard at eroding her self-esteem and forced her to rely upon him. She'd been lucky enough to have a friend like John, who had all but bullied her into protecting her finances, and that had been the saving grace that had allowed her to get on the plane to Ireland. Now, that moment six weeks ago, when she'd stood at the airport and waved goodbye to John, stood out starkly in her mind. She'd been broken and scared, yet... she'd moved forward anyway. What a gift she'd given herself, Iris realized. It wasn't in her nature to walk away from a mess, but she'd done just that. Her world had imploded, and instead of staying there and wallowing in it, day in and day out, she'd lit a match and walked away.

Who knew she had such power?

Fascinated with the woman she now saw in the mirror, Iris reached out and touched a finger to her reflection.

"There you are," Iris whispered. "I've been looking for you."

While her emotions were complicated, Iris realized that she didn't have to figure everything out today. She was too hard on herself, expecting to be capable of processing such huge things in so little time. She'd lost her business. Her boyfriend betrayed her. She'd moved countries. She'd found family. She'd started over. Stupid ex-boyfriend assaulted her.

She's fallen for someone.

That last part made her heart shiver and dance, and she wanted to hold on to that feeling. Of all the emotions that roiled in her gut, that was the one she wanted to grab onto like a life preserver thrown from a boat. She didn't know, not really, if Kane would return her feelings. But he cared for her.

And maybe that was enough to start with. If she could learn to trust someone again, to build a new life together, then just knowing he cared for her, even if it ended up being in friendship only, was an excellent starting point.

The sun was creeping toward the horizon when Iris made her way up the hill to Kane's rental cottage. It was the first day in a long time that no rain had visited Grace's Cove, and she strolled comfortably along in jeans and a T-shirt. She hadn't planned for the number of times someone stopped her on the street to speak with her, which was something new she would have to take into account if she was pressed for time. Iris had never had to budget those things into her schedule when living in a big city.

When she finally reached Kane's cottage, fiery red streaks crisscrossed the sky, and the first star of the evening twinkled brightly in the dusky blue sky. Hearing Kane's voice, Iris detoured around the front door to the back patio area, guessing that he was enjoying the spot of nice weather as well.

"I think the book will be good, like really good, Grant. My readers have been begging to learn more about Prince from Rock Rebels. This is their chance to see what happens with him. I think you're going to be really happy with it," Kane said, speaking into a cell phone at his ear.

Iris stopped in her tracks.

She knew it was terrible to eavesdrop.

Her mother had always warned her about listening in on conversations. It was a part of why she kept her spirit guides muted so much. They often chattered endlessly about all sorts of things they observed, inadvertently giving Iris information she didn't need to hear.

But this? This would have been nice to hear.

From the man himself.

The man she thought she could trust.

Here, she'd bared her life to him in the most humiliating way possible today. He hadn't been writing a screenplay for a television show this whole time.

He was her favorite author.

The author she'd gushed to him about more than once. She referenced the book series enthusiastically when giving him ideas on his latest work. Oh, no…Iris's cheeks flushed crimson. She'd been so silly to think she was helping a budding writer with ideas for his story.

Kane wasn't a budding writer. He didn't need her ideas or her help. He was famous around the world and had a huge following. He was likely rich and went to rich people events like yacht parties and galas. The very idea made Iris shudder.

As the realization that she couldn't trust this man hit her, Iris also quickly understood that there was no way she could fit into his life. Her job and her most recent bad press would be nothing but a detriment to someone like Kane.

No, no…this was never going to work.

The hurt rose to the top of the pile of emotions in her gut, pushing the lightness she had held on to earlier far, far, far down in her gut. When Kane turned, sensing her presence, he paused.

"Grant, I'll call you back."

"You're not Kane. You're K.L. Wallace. Like one of the most famous authors in the world," Iris whispered. The tin of cookies shook in her hands.

"Iris…I was going to tell you, I promise," Kane said, stepping forward, but Iris raised her hands, holding the tin awkwardly.

"I didn't mean to eavesdrop. I brought you cookies," Iris said awkwardly. "To, um, thank you."

"You don't have to thank me," Kane said. He stopped short of touching her, his worried eyes drawn to the bruise on her face. "Iris, please, listen to me."

"No…no, I don't think that I will," Iris surprised

herself by saying. "I think that I heard what I needed to hear. Something that you should have told me a long time ago."

"It's not...I wasn't going to keep it a secret from you forever, Iris. You had a lot on your plate, and once I knew how much you loved the series, I didn't want you to treat me differently. People always do..." Kane trailed off when Iris shoved the tin of cookies into his chest, and he took them from her.

"It's fine, Kane. I mean, it's not. I thought I could trust you, and, like, well, trust is kind of a big thing to me right now. So there's that." Iris laughed and looked away, unable to stare at his too-handsome face any longer. "But it doesn't matter anymore, anyway. We'd never fit, you and me. I think it's best we just stick to what we originally decided. Friends."

"I don't want to be just friends, Iris. And what do you mean we wouldn't fit? That's ridiculous. You've not even given us a chance. From my viewpoint, I'd say we'd fit pretty damn well," Kane protested. He put the tin aside and made to put his arms around Iris, but she put her hand in the air to stop him.

"You don't see it because why would you? You haven't had to fight your whole life for acceptance the way I have. My world and your world don't play together nicely, Kane. Journalists aren't very friendly to my profession."

"And? Why do you think I've kept my name a secret? It's for exactly that reason. I'm not interested in being in the limelight, Iris. I just want to create stories that I love to write. Something that I couldn't do because literally all of my creativity had withered and died until I met you. I was frozen. You brought me back to life, Iris. You. Beautiful, stubborn, brilliant *you*. Please don't throw us in the bin before we've even had a chance to start," Kane asked.

But it was too much.

Perhaps it was the wrong day to learn this. Perhaps it was that Iris maybe just needed to learn to be alone for a while. Either way, she found herself backing away from Kane.

"I'm sorry, Kane. I can't. I just can't. It's best we just…we just…" Iris waved her hand lamely in the air and turned, leaving Kane clenching his fists on the patio behind her.

She didn't know what she walked away from, but Iris knew what she walked toward.

A future in which she put herself first.

CHAPTER 20

*T*hree weeks had passed since Iris had walked away from Kane and, still, he managed to dominate her thoughts. It was frustrating just how often she'd pick up her phone to text him something but then force herself to stop.

Not that it stopped him.

Apparently, the man had decided to take her at her word about being friends and continued to show up every day.

Every day.

It was like being stalked by a golden retriever.

While he didn't help her with as many projects, and Iris drew the line at having him spend too much time in her space, he'd infuriatingly bring her a cup of coffee made just the way she liked it and engage her in mindless chat as though her heart wasn't bleeding for him.

Last week, he'd brought her a fresh batch of spring onions because they were the first thing he'd managed to grow himself and wanted her to have them.

The week before that, he'd brought her a lumpy, misshapen pottery bowl he'd made at the art center down the street. To hold her crystals, he'd said. She'd squirreled it away in her apartment so he couldn't see she was using it and had put it in a place of honor on her windowsill to charge her crystals in the moonlight.

Yesterday, he'd asked her if she thought a group of sharks was called a shiver because they were intimidating. How was she supposed to answer these questions? It was like he'd completely forgotten everything she'd said and carried on like usual.

In front of the whole town, nonetheless.

Since she wasn't letting him in the shop, lest he took up residence and never left, they'd have these conversations on the sidewalk in front of the bookstore. Soon, Iris learned that everyone had become curious about their relationship. Which was exactly what she'd been worried about, Iris fumed, glaring down at the book that Beatrice had left at her front door.

Relationships for Dummies.

"Real funny, Beatrice," Iris called across the landing to where the bookstore door was open. She could just see Bubbles lying in her bed on the counter, her tail swooping lazily.

"I can't imagine what you're talking about," Beatrice called, and Iris pinched her nose before crossing to the front door of the bookshop.

"I don't need this," Iris said, brandishing the book. She laid it on a stack of books by the front counter and danced her fingers down Bubble's back. The cat arched, rolling over, and pawed lightly at Iris's hand.

"Is that right? Seems to me you could use all the help you can get." Beatrice sniffed. Reading glasses perched precariously on her nose as she worked a crossword puzzle.

"I'm doing just fine, thank you very much." Iris was not doing fine, but that was nobody else's business. In fact, Iris was so far from fine that she was starting to wonder if she'd made a huge mistake by coming to Ireland at all.

"You're not. You've got dark circles under your eyes, and you've been avoiding the pub, much to Cait's annoyance. The woman is ready to come down and drag you out of your hole. You're losing weight. I know heartbreak when I see it."

"It's not...I'm just..." Iris sighed. She was hanging on by a thread these days and hated how heartsick she felt. She'd made the decision to walk away, hadn't she? And it was a smart one. For both of them. Why couldn't anyone see that? "I'm busy putting the finishing touches on everything. I'm also buried in all the paperwork that goes with opening a business in another country. Visa, residency, licensing, opening a bank account. It's not like I can waltz in here, set up a table on the street corner, and take cash for payment."

"No, that's not really an option, is it? Sure, and I can certainly understand why setting up a business takes so much of your time. But that's not what has you losing sleep at night, is it, honey?"

At Beatrice's term of endearment, tears pricked Iris's eyes.

"It doesn't matter anymore, Beatrice. It won't work.

Why can't everyone just accept that so I, no we, can move forward?"

"Because from where I'm standing, you are the only one standing in your way."

Would it be wrong to tackle an old woman? Or maybe just kick her a few times and run? Iris narrowed her eyes as she thought about it.

"Don't give me that look. I'm stronger than you think, girlie." Beatrice pushed her glasses up on her nose and marked another word down on her puzzle. "Why don't you take the afternoon off? My car's out back. Go for a drive. You haven't left the shop in weeks. If you don't want to socialize, then go be in nature. It has a mighty restorative effect, you know."

"I...actually, you know what? I'll take you up on that. Are you sure you don't mind?" Iris agreed, simply to get away from her nagging for the afternoon.

"Keys are right there." Beatrice pointed at where a set of keys hung on a hook by the counter.

"I'll be back before dark."

Beatrice waved her on, nibbling on her pencil as she stared at her crossword, and Iris felt the first bit of excitement she'd felt in a while. Maybe she had been working too hard. A break wouldn't kill her.

Soon enough, Iris was driving the sporty little sedan along the narrow road that led toward Gracie's house. Iris had thought to visit the nature center or something of the like, but she'd forgotten about the whole driving on the other side of the road. Now she gripped the wheel tightly and muttered curses until she saw the turnoff for the cove. Swinging the car along the dirt path, Iris let out a sigh of relief. Her back was damp with sweat, and she could've kicked herself for not remembering how precarious the drive was. Getting out, she dragged herself to the picnic table and plopped down, her chest heaving as she waited for nature to work its supposed miracle on her.

The cove took her breath away.

Today, the sun's rays hit the water at such an angle that it almost looked like it was lit from within, reminding Iris of the time she had seen it glow. She'd forgotten about that but made a mental note to ask Gracie if that was a magickal thing with the cove or not. But today, the bright turquoise color was simply nature showing off. Despite her mood, Iris found the tension loosening at her shoulders. A healthy breeze caused the wildflowers along the cliff's edge to dance in the wind, bobbing their sunny yellow heads to some unknown beat. A few birds swooped and dove into the water far below.

It wasn't surprising that Grace O'Malley had chosen this spot for her death. It was a place for endings and beginnings. Birth and death. Old and new.

Could she do the same for herself? Iris wondered if she could leave her past behind in Boston and truly start fresh here. Or if old wounds would always crack open, bleeding on those around her.

"I'm sorry I didn't warn you sooner."

"For fu…" Iris cut off a curse and held her hand to her chest, turning to see Fiona walking toward her. "Is this fun for you? Just scaring people by popping up unannounced?"

"It can be." Fiona smiled. "I particularly like to annoy Gracie."

"Oh, I bet she takes that well." Iris grinned, thinking

about firebrand Gracie and how she'd react to being startled constantly.

"She does not. Which is why I keep doing it. Good to keep that girl on her toes."

"What are you apologizing for?" Iris crossed her arms over her chest and watched as Fiona looked out over the water.

"For not warning you sooner about that awful man. I came as soon as I could."

"It's fine. Bruises fade." Iris shrugged, not wanting to talk about Warren again.

"Physical bruises fade," Fiona amended. Turning, she looked down at Iris. "Why did you buy Aislinn's painting? Of the cove?"

"I…" Iris sighed. "I just knew it was mine. I don't know, I liked it, I guess?"

"Go deeper," Fiona suggested.

That seemed to be what everyone around her was nudging her to do lately and, frankly, it was getting kind of annoying. That being said, it wasn't every day that she chatted with a ghost on a cliff, so perhaps she needed to pay attention to the messages the universe kept trying to send her.

"It felt like coming home. Like…a cleansing of sorts. Like I could be me, in this place, so long as I trusted…"

"Trusted what?"

"Myself." Iris blinked at the water.

"*The Beginning*," Fiona said. "An apt title, no?"

"It is. I want to be the person I believed I could be when I saw that painting for the first time."

"What's stopping you?"

"*Me.* I'm stopping me." Iris laughed, annoyed that Beatrice was right.

"What do you want, Iris? If you had your perfect day with no restrictions?"

"I want to open my shop. Here. In Grace's Cove. I want to wave to my neighbors. I want to read for my clients. I want to have a pint in the pub and wake up next to Kane. Oh…" Iris's heart caught at the thought of waking up next to Kane.

"Why can't you have that? All of that?" Fiona asked.

"Because I don't know if it would work out."

"So why bother trying at all?" Fiona guessed.

"Something like that."

"Is it worth it? Losing him?" Fiona nodded to the water, where that weird blue light shimmered again. "You saw that, didn't you?"

"I did…do you know…what does it mean?" Iris stood, crossing to the cliff's edge to stare at the glowing water. She gasped when it winked out.

"It only shines in the presence of true love." Fiona chuckled. "Well, and when I make it do that. But I was just showing off there. I wanted to know if you'd seen it yet."

"I have." Iris gulped, her heart hammering in her chest.

"And who were you with at the time?" Fiona turned to her.

"Kane," Iris whispered.

"The cove doesn't lie. But you do. To yourself. If you're going to go after your new beginning, then do so with honesty, Iris. The truth always has a way of catching up with us."

With that, Fiona winked out of sight, but Iris was

already heading for the car. There was no way Beatrice could have known where Iris would go today, but the woman had been right–being in nature had absolutely clarified her direction. It just took the help of a ghost and a little extra magick as well.

By the time Iris returned to the village, once again coated in sweat, she was torn on whether she should drive straight to Kane's or drop the car off first. But she didn't know if Beatrice would need the car for anything, and in the interest of being a good neighbor, she went home first.

"Here are your keys," Iris called, knocking on Beatrice's apartment door.

"Oh, one moment." Beatrice opened the door shortly with a brown box in her hands. "Did you have a nice afternoon then?"

"It was lovely. I think you were right. Nature is what I needed."

"I'm always right, dear. Now, your young man came by but didn't want to leave this outside, so I promised to give it to you the minute you got home."

"What is it?" Iris exchanged the keys for the box, looking down at the simple brown package like it was a bomb.

"I have no clue. I'm nosy, but I'm not rude. You'll tell me, of course, once you've opened it?" Beatrice's eyes gleamed with interest.

"I promise. Well, unless it's sex toys or something." Iris winked.

"Like I don't know what those are?" Beatrice chuckled and closed the door at Iris's surprised look.

"Too much information." Iris shook her head and

unlocked her apartment door. Throwing her purse on the table, she flipped on her lights. She proceeded directly to her bedroom to plop down on the bed, which was still the only comfortable piece of furniture in the house.

It wasn't unusual for Kane to bring her a gift, so she wasn't sure why her hands trembled as she lifted the lid from the box.

Her heart skipped a beat.

Inside, reams of typed pages sat, neatly clipped at the top. A handwritten note was affixed to the first page.

Iris,

I've finished my book. The book that you helped me write. Nobody has seen this story yet. Not my editor, not my agent. It is completely untouched for you to do what you want with. I'm giving you this to read, rip up, or leak to the entire world if you want to do so. I hope you don't, but I'll respect your decision. You see, I trust you. Not only with my book but also with my heart. You hold my future in your hands, both professionally and personally.

When I met you, Iris, I was a broken man. And you, with your beautiful light, shone through my cracks and warmed my soul. You saw me for me, and you didn't turn away. Instead, you lifted me up, cheered me on, and made me laugh every day. And I see you for you, Iris. You have such a pure heart, and you're so incredibly brave. You didn't even realize that you lent me some of your courage. I needed it, and maybe I still do.

I miss you like crazy, Iris. Please...

Just...please.

Love,
Kane

TEARS DRIPPED DOWN HER CHEEKS, and she moved the box hastily away from her lap so they wouldn't get on the manuscript. Flipping Kane's note up, Iris sobbed even harder when she saw the book's name.

The One Where She Rescues the Prince.

CHAPTER 21

*K*ane didn't sleep.

It had been over twelve hours since he'd dropped his book off at Iris's apartment, and still he hadn't heard a word. He paced his living room, uncertain what to do with his free time now that the book was finished and unable to move forward.

Ideas were no longer the issue. It was like a dam had broken, and so many new book plots flooded his brain that all he could do was try to catch the threads of them before they were lost forever. His tattered notebook was filled to the brim with new characters and plot twists, so, in theory, he should be able to sit down and write.

But still he paced, waiting.

Waiting was a horrible thing, wasn't it? How many people spent their life waiting? Waiting to take a chance? Waiting to start over? Waiting for love? Maybe the real lesson here was that Kane couldn't wait anymore. Instead, he had to make his life happen for himself. Decision made, Kane grabbed his keys and strode to the door. He was done waiting on Iris. She would have to give him a clear answer, one way or the other, on if they could have a future together.

Swinging his door open, Kane shouted in surprise, and Iris squeaked, almost dropping the box with the manuscript she held. Catching the box, Kane grabbed her arm and wrenched her inside, slamming the door behind her before she could escape.

"You scared me," Iris gasped, holding a hand on her chest over her heart.

She looked wonderful. Heartbreakingly, achingly, lovely. Dark circles smudged the delicate skin beneath her eyes, and she wore a tattered sweatshirt pulled on over paint-smudged leggings. Her hair was piled high on top of her head, the red having started to fade into more of a strawberry-blond color. Kane had never seen anyone more beautiful.

"Sorry...I was fed up with waiting on you. I was coming to you. Even if I had to stand outside your apartment and sing a song at the top of my lungs like some heartbroken teenager from an eighties movie."

"Hmm, I'd like to see that, I think." Iris's gaze shot to the door, a calculating look in her eyes. "I could just run home, and you can still give it a go."

Kane blocked the door with his shoulders, narrowing his eyes at her.

"Not a chance, doll. You missed that opportunity."

"I knew I should have waited a little longer." Iris sighed. Turning, she walked toward the kitchen, spun once more, and crossed the living room. She paced, just like Kane did when he was upset, and he watched her carefully, his heart hammering in his chest. Kane wondered what was going on in that maddeningly fascinating brain of hers.

"I read your book," Iris said, breaking the silence that had grown taut with unsaid words.

"And?" Kane asked, hope blooming low in his gut.

"I stayed up all night, Kane. I couldn't put it down. It…" Iris held a hand to her heart. "It captivated me. Enchanted me. I'm…addicted. To the story. To you. To your words. To how you see me," Iris said. Her voice caught, and a sheen of tears touched her eyes. And still, Kane waited. "I know I wasn't the character in your book, yet. Yet… I could see. You were writing to me, weren't you? You think that I…" Iris stilled and turned once more, her fists clenched at her sides. Kane let her pace, the silence growing longer, and waited for her to decide their future. She whirled.

"Is that how you see me?" Iris demanded. "That I…I saved you? You? Of all people? A world-renowned author who…"

"Who was broken and battered and barely treading water when he met you." Kane prowled forward, took her hands so tightly clenched, and brought them to his heart. "Months I'd been lost. Longer than that, if I'm being honest with myself. And then you came along in your life raft and saved a drowning man."

"I don't know if I want that responsibility. What if you were just ready to move on? What if it had been any woman you'd met in the airport?" Iris blinked up at him, worry dancing in her eyes.

"Ah, darling, it wouldn't have been. Fate wouldn't let

that happen to us." Kane raised her hands to his lips, kissing each one gently. "What do your guides say?"

Iris muttered something that sounded suspiciously like "do him," and Kane chuckled.

"What was that? I couldn't quite hear you."

"Nothing." Iris glowered at him and stepped back. Reaching up, she pulled her bag from her shoulder, put it on his desk, and dug in it. "I have something for you."

"You don't need to…" Kane trailed off when Iris turned, her beloved pair of purple boots in her hands.

"I do. These are for you. I know it may seem silly, and you can't wear them or anything, but…it's the meaning, okay?" Iris said, a challenge in her eyes.

Kane remembered what she'd said about her boots and instantly understood the meaning behind her gift. Warmth flooded him, making him almost dizzy with anticipation.

"I understand," Kane said, his voice soft with love for her. This darling, stubborn, beautiful woman.

"I love these boots…" Iris cleared her throat before continuing. "Because…they support me. They make me smile. They're comfortable to wear. And…"

"They make you feel pretty," Kane finished, reciting her words.

"You remember." Iris blinked up at him, frozen for a moment. Kane waited her out, knowing she'd have to take the first step. "And…and. Well, I don't need them anymore, you see? Because I have you to make me feel that way."

There it was.

Kane swooped in, removing the boots from her hands and placing them gently by his computer before scooping

Iris up, much to her surprise and giggled protests. Before she could complain too much, he dropped her unceremoniously on his bed and pounced, pinning her arms above her head so he could claim her mouth with his.

It was the kiss of all kisses.

Both a beginning and an ending.

And when he loved her that night, Kane finally understood what his heart had been trying to tell him all along.

There can be no ending without a new beginning. Such was the cyclical nature of life. If he didn't let go, he'd never step forward. And so, that night, with Iris in his arms and his heart wide open, Kane gave himself over to the joy of beginning.

EPILOGUE

"*I* can't believe I'm finally going to open next week," Iris said. Beaming, she turned in a circle, still feeling giddy about what a one-eighty her life had taken. Yet, in some respects, she'd come full circle, hadn't she? She had her shop, albeit a prettier and upgraded one, in a far more interesting location, and she was still in a relationship. Albeit also with an upgraded model, Iris mused as Kane came into the store brandishing a hammer and nails.

"Sorry, I just had to grab my tools." Kane flexed for her, and Iris giggled. It turned out that she was a giggler, something that still astonished her. Perhaps she just needed to be with the right person.

"Construction Kane is really sexy," Iris agreed, making appropriate oohing and aahing sounds as he flexed again with a hammer in hand.

The shop was finished. The midnight blue looked perfect on the painted wall, highlighting the warm red brick of the other walls and bringing out the honey tones of the wood floors. The mismatched rugs, eclectic thrift décor, and charming vintage lamps created the shop's cool yet relaxed ambience. Every morning, she walked the room, still delighted with what she'd created here.

It was crazy how, when Warren had betrayed her, she'd been convinced that her life was over. Now, she realized his betrayal had only been the beginning. That was why, today, they were finally going to hang Aislinn's beautiful painting, the first piece of art she'd purchased when she'd arrived in Grace's Cove. Iris had promised herself she would hang the painting in a prized spot on the wall when she was ready to open her doors to the public.

The Beginning.

It had been so much more for her than that, but Iris still was awed at how that painting, and the title, had managed to become such a prominent theme in her life. Turning, she smiled and...

"Kane! What are you doing?" Iris demanded.

Kane smiled patiently at her from where he kneeled on the floor, holding a ring box in his hand. Iris's heart skipped a beat, and her hands fluttered weakly at her chest as she looked down at him in shock. It was too soon. Was it too soon? She kept her spirit guides on mute, only wanting to listen to her own guidance as she stepped forward.

"I'm hanging a painting. What does it look like?" Kane rolled his eyes, and Iris snorted. Of course he would make her laugh in the middle of a proposal. That was just who he was. Goofy, funny, incredibly sexy, and unendingly patient with her.

"Oh well, by all means, don't let me stop you then." Iris blinked as tears filled her eyes.

"Iris…I don't want you to think I'm proposing right here and now because I have to be a part of the shop. This is your baby and your business. I promise I'll cheer you on as much as you need, but I'll never try to rule it for you. But, at the same time, knowing what this painting means to you, well…it just felt right. I love you so very much, Iris Moon Dillon. My stubborn, fascinating, prickly, beautiful woman. I have a very important question for you…"

"Okay." Iris swallowed.

"Will you be my new beginning? And my last?" Kane asked, his eyes warm with love.

"Yes, oh, of course I will, Kane. We're meant to be, you and I, aren't we?" Iris gasped when he flipped the box open, revealing a purple amethyst surrounded heavily by diamonds. "Oh, Kane…purple like my boots."

"I took a chance there…if you don't like—" Iris cut off his words with her lips, all but crawling into his lap as they tumbled to the floor, knowing he would catch her. Because that was what Kane did. He caught her, lifted her, and showed her just what life could be like with a true partner. It was a beautiful thing, loving Kane, and she didn't care about anything else.

"I thought we were hanging a painting, not having an orgy," Beatrice griped from the door, and Iris broke away from Kane's kiss, laughter on her lips. Bubbles ran across the floor and swatted at Kane with her paw, and Kane raised an eyebrow at Iris.

"I warned you about cats, didn't I?"

"She's just protective of me, isn't she?" Iris cooed, scratching Bubbles under the chin before rolling awkwardly off Kane and helping him to stand. She beamed as he slid the ring on her finger, ignoring Beatrice's gasp of surprise, and wrapped her arms around Kane's shoulder, savoring another kiss with him.

"Well, now, I wouldn't have brought up orgies if I knew you'd just proposed," Beatrice huffed. Iris turned, pressing her cheek to Kane's chest, hearing his laughter echo hers as more people crowded through the front door.

"Who is having an orgy? I thought this was a surprise party?" Gracie demanded.

"Did you throw me a party?" Iris asked, pulling back to look up at Kane.

"Well, I'd meant to help you hang the painting and then drag you upstairs after my awesome proposal, and then everyone was supposed to come in and set up for a surprise party," Kane said, narrowing his eyes at Gracie.

"You proposed?" Gracie shrieked, ignoring Kane's annoyance, and descended upon them both. Soon, Iris was surrounded by what felt like the whole town as everyone passed drinks, admired the ring, and hugged each of them. It was overwhelming, chaotic, and totally out of either of their hands. Yet somehow there was beauty in the messiness of living in a community that insisted on being involved in their business whether they liked it or not.

This was family now, Iris realized, looking around at the party that was now in full swing. She shouted, raising her arms, and someone shut off the little speaker blasting music.

"Thank you all for coming to my surprise party, and well, surprise proposal, I guess?" Iris beamed down at her ring, sparkling on her finger, and then up at Kane as he came to her side. "I had promised myself when I was ready to open the shop that I would hang this stunning painting from our resident genius artist–Aislinn." Cheers went up as Aislinn bowed in the corner.

"The name of the painting is *The Beginning*. And I think the title is so very apt for so many reasons. Not the least of which is all of you. Being here for me, tonight, and showing me that I can start over, that I can rise, that I can still do the things that I love surrounded by a community who will support me. I'm humbled to have your support, and I'd be grateful for you to witness the hanging of this priceless piece of art."

Everyone in the room cheered and quieted as Kane took out his hammer.

"A little to the left," Iris said.

"Are you certain?" Kane asked.

"Oh boyo, just do as she says. You'll get used to it soon enough," someone quipped from the audience.

"She's the boss. It's her business," Kane said, his eyes steady on Iris's. "She can hang it any way she wants. I just want to make her happy."

"Aw," Gracie called. "Don't make me ruin my makeup."

"You make me happy," Iris beamed at Kane. "And thank you for listening to me. Yes, that's the perfect spot."

With that, Kane hammered two nails into the wall and hung the painting with a dramatic flourish. Iris stepped back, her hands at her heart, and beamed at the beautiful depiction of the cove. The light from above highlighted the colors of the sea just right, and the dark paint on the wall behind it made the painting stand out like the showstopper it was.

"Sorry, I'm late," Cait called as she came through the door, a leather book in hand. "But I had to run back to the pub when I heard the news."

"What are you talking about?" Iris asked, accepting a kiss on the cheek as Cait breezed past, immediately commanding the room much like she did her pub.

"Who won, Cait?" Gracie called.

"Who won what?" Iris asked, narrowing her eyes as Cait flopped the book on the table and paged through it.

"I think we're about to find out just how close the town is," Kane said. He put an arm around Iris's shoulder, pulling her in close, and Iris warmed at his touch.

"Did they bet…on us?" Iris asked, looking up at Kane, torn between annoyance and surprise.

"Looks to be that way," Kane said.

"You proposed today?" Cait looked over her reading glasses at Kane, a stern look on her face.

"Yes, ma'am. Are you needing the exact time? The weather? The phase of the moon?" Kane asked.

"Cheeky one, isn't he?" Cait raised an eyebrow and returned to her book, trailing her finger down the page.

"Is this a thing that the Irish do?" Iris asked, honestly bewildered at what was going on.

"Not as a tradition, no, though we do like a wager here and there, I won't lie."

"Ah, perfect," Cait beamed. Looking around the room, she waved. "Congrats to Beatrice!"

"Well, sure and I must be dreaming!" Beatrice squealed and clapped her hands. "I never win anything."

"It's your lucky night. I've got your winnings up at the pub. You'll be making your way up there, won't you?" Cait asked, slamming the book closed and turning. It was more of an order than a question. With that, she breezed back out, and people followed her like the Grand Dame she was.

"We could stay behind and..." Kane whispered a particularly dirty suggestion in Iris's ear, and lust pooled low in her stomach.

"That's for later, you two. It's time to celebrate with me." Beatrice hooked Iris's arm and dragged her to the front door, surprising a laugh out of Iris. "You'll have enough time for that later. It's only just the beginning, after all."

Iris's eyes caught on the painting as she locked the shop door, her new family surrounding her on the sidewalk, and she smiled. Unmuting her spirit guides, she listened and was surprised when silence greeted her.

Turning, she stepped into her future.

SPEAKING OF NEW BEGINNINGS...I cannot tell you how excited I am to share with you a sneak peek at a brand-new series. The Scotsman insisted it was time for me to write a few stories based on his glorious homeland, and I think you'll love this new series as much as I do. Plus, who doesn't love handsome Scotsmen in kilts? I know that I do! Read on for an excerpt.

DYING for just a taste more of Iris & Kane - download the bonus scene to see a glimpse into their future!

Visit my website to download:
https://www.triciaomalley.com/free

WILD SCOTTISH KNIGHT

BOOK 1 IN THE ENCHANTED HIGHLANDS SERIES

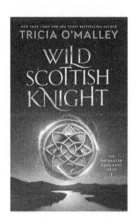

Opposites attract in this modern-day fairytale when American, Sophie MacKnight, inherits a Scottish castle along with a hot grumpy Scotsman who is tasked with training her to be a magickal knight to save the people of Loren Brae.

*W*hat was it about death that brought out the worst in people? Most of those at the celebration of life today hadn't spoken to my uncle in years, and now I was being showered with rabid curiosity dressed up as forced condolences. Let's be honest. Uncle Arthur had been filthy rich, and everybody was here for the READING OF THE WILL. Yes, I heard it like that in all-caps whenever someone asked me about the READING OF THE WILL. I barely suppressed a hysterical giggle as I envisioned a small man with a heralding trumpet, standing on the balcony and unfurling a long roll of paper, reading off the terms of THE WILL like Oprah during her Christmas specials. *And you get a car...and you get a boat...*

I was currently winning the bet on how many times my uncle's ex-wives would try to console me, a fact which simultaneously cheered and annoyed me. There were seven wives in total, having multiplied like Gremlins being exposed to water, before his last, and my favorite, had cured my uncle of his marrying hastily habit.

Bagpipes sounded behind me, and though I wasn't usually a nervous sort, my drink went flying. Turning, I glared at the bagpiper who had the gall to wink at me. Cheeky bastard, I thought, narrowing my eyes as he confidently strode past, parting the crowd like a hot knife through butter. Suitably impressed, because the bagpipe was the type of instrument that demanded attention, my eyes followed the man as he crossed the lawn, kilt billowing in the wind.

"Damn it, Sophie." Wife Number Two glared at me and dabbed at her tweed jacket in sharp motions. "This is Chanel." The only thing tighter than the woman's severe bun was her grasp on my uncle's alimony. Before I could apologize, Number Two strode off, snapping her finger at a caterer, her lips no doubt pursed in disapproval. Only my uncle would plan and cater his own funeral. I grabbed another glass of champagne from the tray of a passing waiter.

Arthur MacKnight, of Knight's Protective Services, leader in home and commercial security systems worldwide, did not leave anything to chance. His attention-to-detail, pragmatic attitude, and strong code of ethics had rocketed his company to the top of the list. On the personal side? Arthur had been a known eccentric, disgustingly wealthy, and one of my favorite people. With a ten-figure company on the line, I guess I couldn't blame people for wanting to know the contents of THE WILL. But not me. I didn't care about the money. I just wanted my uncle back.

"Prissy old scarecrow," Lottie MacKnight whispered in my ear. As the proud owner of the title of Wife Number Seven, Lottie had withstood the test of time and had made Arthur very happy in his later years. She was creative, quirky, and the most down to earth of all the wives, and I had bonded with her instantly over our shared hatred of fancy restaurants. I still remembered giggling over a plate that had been delivered with much finesse but carried little more than a sliver of carrot with a puff of foam. Arthur had looked on, amusement dancing in his eyes, as his new wife and only niece had tried to maintain their composure in front of the stuffy maître d'.

When I was twelve, I had come home one day to the contents of my bedroom being placed in boxes by our very apologetic housekeeper. Much to my horror, my parents had informed me—via a note on the kitchen counter, mind you—that I was leaving for boarding school that same evening. Somehow, Lottie had caught wind of it and rescued me, bringing me back home to live with her and Arthur. I'd happily settled into a life of contradictions—business lessons at breakfast, fencing lessons at lunch, and magick studies after dinner. Well, not magick per se, but Arthur had nourished an insatiable love for myths, legends, and the unexplainable.

Once a year, I dutifully endured a phone call with my parents from whatever far-flung destination they were visiting. As an afterthought, I would occasionally receive inappropriate birthday gifts that would leave me blinking in confusion. A few we kept, for the sheer madness of it all, like the gold-plated two-foot penguin statue. Lottie had promptly named it Mooshy, set him in the front hall, and put little hats or bows on him depending on the occasion. Because of them, my tender teenage years had gone from stilted and awkward to vibrant and fulfilled, and I would forever be grateful.

Arthur's loss numbed me, like someone had cut out the part of me where my feelings were supposed to reside, and now I was just shambling about making awkward small talk with people who were suddenly very interested in speaking with me. Even the Old Wives Club, as Lottie and I referred to the other six wives, had made weak attempts at mothering me. Hence the bet I'd made with Lottie. Upon arrival at the funeral, the wives had besieged me, like a murder of crows dressed in couture, angry in the way of perpetually hungry people. Lottie, being Lottie, had swooped forward in her colorful caftan and flower fascinator, rescuing me from the wives by cheerfully suggesting they look for the attorney who carried THE WILL. The Old Wives Club had pivoted as one, like a squadron of fighter planes, and narrowed in on the beleaguered attorney with ruthless efficiency.

The funeral was being held on the back lawn of Arthur's estate in California, his castle towering over the proceedings. Yes, *castle*. Arthur had built his house to remind him of the castles in Scotland, much to the chagrin of the neighborhood. His neighbors, their houses all sleek lines and modern angles, had hated Arthur's castle. I *loved* it. What was the point of earning all that money if you couldn't have fun with it? Arthur had nourished a deep affection for his Scottish roots, often traveling there several times a year, and had spent many a night trying to convince me to enjoy what he claimed were the finest of Scottish whiskies. As far as I was concerned, if that was the best Scotland could do, then I was not impressed.

It was one of those perpetually cheerful California days, and the sun threatened to burn my fair skin. Arthur had always joked that he could get a sunburn walking to the mailbox and back. He wasn't far off. I'd already wished I had brought a hat with me. Instead, I slid my bargain-bin sunglasses on my nose to dull the light. Designer sunglasses were a no-go for me. At the rate I sat on my sunglasses and broke them, it was far more economical for me to grab some from the rack on the way out of the gas station.

"Nice glasses. Dior?" Wife Number Three drifted up, her knuckles tight on the martini glass she held.

"No, um, BP," I nodded. I pronounced it as Bay-Pay, skewing the name of the gas station.

"Hmm, I haven't heard of them. I'll be sure to look for their show this spring in Paris. Darlings!" Number Three fluttered her fingers at a fancy couple and left to air-kiss her way into an invitation to a yacht party.

"Break another pair of sunglasses?" Lottie asked, biting into a cube of cheese. There was cheese? I looked around for the waiter who carried that coveted tray and grinned.

"Third this week."

"That's a lot for you." Lottie turned to me, her eyes searching my face. "You okay, sweetie? This is a tough time for us. I loved Arthur, and I'll miss him like crazy, but it's different for you. He was like…"

"My father," I whispered, spying across the lawn my parents who had arrived over an hour ago and still hadn't bothered to greet their only daughter. Their indifference to my existence still shouldn't sting…and *yet*. Here we were. I tried to frame it in my head like they were just people that I used to room with back in the day.

"And as your mother"—Lottie waved a jewel-encrusted hand at my parents—"I don't care that those two idiots are here. *I'm* claiming Mama rights. So, as your mother, I want to make sure you'll be able to grieve properly. I'm here for you, you know."

"I know, I know." I pressed a kiss to Lottie's cheek,

catching the faint scent of soap and turpentine. Lottie must have been painting her moods again. She was a world-renowned painter in her own right and worked through her emotions on her canvasses. All of Arthur's and my spreadsheets and business talk had made her eyes glaze over with boredom. "I don't really know yet how to think or feel. I'm numb, if I'm being honest."

"Numb is just fine. As Pink Floyd would attest to…it's a comfortable place to be. Just live in that space for a little bit and we'll handle what comes. What about Chad? Or is it Chet?" Lottie affected a confused expression, though I knew very well she knew my boyfriend's name.

My boyfriend, Chad, was good-looking in a polished private school kind of way, and at first I'd just been drawn to someone who'd paid careful attention to me. Now, as I watched him schmooze my parents—*not that he knew they were my parents*—I felt an odd sort of detachment from him. Perhaps that was grief numbing my feelings. Or maybe I liked the idea of a Chad more than an actual Chad himself.

"He's been very supportive," I told Lottie. Which was true. Chad had doted on me constantly since Arthur had died, but so had all my new besties that had crawled out of the woodwork upon the news of Arthur's death. Lottie patted my arm and turned as the celebrant began speaking.

The words flowed over me, intertwining and blurring together, as my own memories of Arthur flashed through my mind. Our heated fencing battles—a sport Arthur had insisted I learn—his quirky obsession with all things Scottish, his willingness to always listen to any new ideas I had for the company, and the way he'd always called me his wee lassie. No, I wasn't ready to say goodbye.

"Oh, shit." Lottie gripped my arm, her fingers digging into the soft flesh, and I pulled myself from my thoughts to see what had distracted Lottie.

The bagpiper had returned to the back of the crowd, having circled the lawn, and now stood waiting for the celebrant's signal. Behind him, Arthur's five Scottish Terriers tumbled about.

"Did you let the dogs out?" I whispered, horror filling me. Arthur's Scotty dogs, while decidedly adorable, were quite simply put—terrors.

"No, I didn't. But the lawyer had asked where they were…" Understanding dawned and we turned to each other.

"Arthur," I said, shaking my head.

"That *crazy* man. God, I loved him." Lottie brushed at a tear as the wail of bagpipes began again and the kilted man once more strode forward.

Amazing Grace. For one haunting moment, the music transported me to another time where I could just imagine a Scottish warrior crossing the land in search of his love. Romantic thoughts which had no place here, I reminded myself, fixated on the bagpiper. The dogs bounced after the man like he was a Scottish Pied Piper, and only then did I see that one of them carried a large stuffed Highland cow. *Coo*, I automatically corrected myself. A heiland coo had been one of Arthur's favorite things to photograph on his travels to Scotland, and he'd even talked of developing a Coo-finder App so that the tourists could more easily get their own photographs.

"You don't think…" A thought occurred to me, but it was so ridiculous I couldn't bring myself to say it.

"Nothing that man did surprised me." Lottie chuckled. We watched with horrified fascination as the dogs reached the front of the funeral gathering. The Old Wives Club shifted in unison, likely due to the possibility of getting dog hair on their Chanel, and I couldn't look away from the impending doom. It was like watching a couple fight in public—I knew it was bad to eavesdrop, but I always wanted to listen and pick whose side I was on. Spoiler alert. I usually sided with the woman.

"Tavish and Bruce always fight over toys," I hissed as two of the dogs separated themselves from the pack, their ears flattening.

"Arthur knows…*knew* that," Lottie said, her hand still gripping my arm. I winced as it tightened. A gasp escaped me when the dogs leapt at each other. Houston, we have a problem.

A flurry of barking exploded as the last notes of *Amazing Grace* faded into the sun and the bagpiper strolled away seemingly unconcerned with the chaos he left in his wake. Maybe he was used to it, for the Scots *could* be unruly at times, and this was just another day's work for him. I grimaced as Tavish and Bruce got ahold of the coo, each gripping a leg, and pulled with all their might. The celebrant, uncertain of what to do, walked forward and made shooing gestures with his hands.

The dogs ignored him, turning in a manic circle, whipping their heads back and forth as they enjoyed a fabulous game of tug. Growls and playful barks carried over the stunned silence of the gathering, with everyone at a loss of how to proceed.

With one giant rip, Bruce won the toy from Tavish and streaked through the horrified crowd. A fine white powder exploded from the coo, coating the Old Wives Club, and spraying the front line.

"His ashes," I breathed. My heart skipped a beat.

"Indeed," Lottie murmured.

Bruce broke from the crowd and tore across the lawn toward the cliffs, the rest of the dogs in hot pursuit, a doggy version of Braveheart. Tavish threw his head back and howled, and I was certain I could just make out the cry for "freeeeedom" on the wind.

The wind that now carried a cloud of ashes back to the funeral gathering.

Pandemonium broke out as the crowd raced for the castle, trying to beat the ash cloud, while Lottie and I stood upwind to observe the chaos from afar. A muffled snort had me turning my head.

"You can't possibly be..." I trailed off as Lottie pressed her lips together in vain, another snort escaping. To my deep surprise, the numb space inside of me unlocked long enough for amusement to trickle in. In moments, we were bent at the waist, howling with laughter, while the Old Wives Club shot us death glares from across the lawn.

"Oh." Lottie straightened and wiped tears from her eyes. "Arthur would've loved that."

I wrapped an arm around Lottie and watched Wife Number Three vomit into a bush.

"It's almost like he planned it." As soon as I said the

words, I *knew* he had. Raising my champagne glass to the sky in acknowledgement, I felt the first bands of grief unknot inside me. He'd wanted us to laugh, as his last parting gift, to remember that in the face of it all…the ridiculous was worth celebrating.

Wild Scottish Knight
Book 1 in the Enchanted Highlands series

AUTHOR'S NOTE

As always, it's a delight to visit Grace's Cove again. I had no idea when I first started writing this series that it would span twelve books as well as generate two spin-off series. It's amazing, isn't it, where our dreams will guide us? I can't say what is next for the Mystic Cove series, as I'm currently deeply in love with writing something new: The Enchanted Highland series. I polled my lovely readers to ask what their favorite elements from the Mystic Cove books were, and then I took those favorite pieces and sprinkled them into this new series. I can't even begin to tell you how excited I am about this next series, and I hope you'll fall in love with Loren Brae as much as you have with Grace's Cove. I suspect, if you're anything like me, you'll love having a whole new world of friends to visit. Plus, there are hot men in kilts, and one of them owns a kilt-wearing chihuahua. I mean, you know you want to find out what that's about, don't you?

So hop on the ferry with me, and we'll travel from the

Emerald Isles to the wilds of the Scottish Highlands, where romance and myths intertwine to form your new favorite series. Enjoy!

THE ISLE OF DESTINY SERIES

ALSO BY TRICIA O'MALLEY

Stone Song

Sword Song

Spear Song

Sphere Song

A completed series.

Available in audio, e-book & paperback!

"Love this series. I will read this multiple times. Keeps you on the edge of your seat. It has action, excitement and romance all in one series."

- Amazon Review

THE WILDSONG SERIES

ALSO BY TRICIA O'MALLEY

Song of the Fae

Melody of Flame

Chorus of Ashes

"The magic of Fae is so believable. I read these books in one sitting and can't wait for the next one. These are books you will reread many times."

- Amazon Review

Available in audio, e-book & paperback!

Available Now

THE SIREN ISLAND SERIES

ALSO BY TRICIA O'MALLEY

Good Girl

Up to No Good

A Good Chance

Good Moon Rising

Too Good to Be True

A Good Soul

In Good Time

A completed series.

Available in audio, e-book & paperback!

"Love her books and was excited for a totally new and different one! Once again, she did NOT disappoint! Magical in multiple ways and on multiple levels. Her writing style, while similar to that of Nora Roberts, kicks it up a notch!! I want to visit that island, stay in the B&B and meet the gals who run it! The characters are THAT real!!!" - Amazon Review

THE ALTHEA ROSE SERIES

ALSO BY TRICIA O'MALLEY

One Tequila

Tequila for Two

Tequila Will Kill Ya (Novella)

Three Tequilas

Tequila Shots & Valentine Knots (Novella)

Tequila Four

A Fifth of Tequila

A Sixer of Tequila

Seven Deadly Tequilas

Eight Ways to Tequila

Tequila for Christmas (Novella)

"Not my usual genre but couldn't resist the Florida Keys setting. I was hooked from the first page. A fun read with just the right amount of crazy! Will definitely follow this series."- Amazon Review

A completed series.

Available in audio, e-book & paperback!

ALSO BY TRICIA O'MALLEY

STAND ALONE NOVELS

Ms. Bitch

"Ms. Bitch is sunshine in a book! An uplifting story of fighting your way through heartbreak and making your own version of happily-ever-after."

~Ann Charles, USA Today Bestselling Author

Starting Over Scottish

Grumpy. Meet Sunshine.

She's American. He's Scottish. She's looking for a fresh start. He's returning to rediscover his roots.

One Way Ticket

A funny and captivating beach read where booking a one-way ticket to paradise means starting over, letting go, and taking a chance on love…one more time

10 out of 10 - The BookLife Prize

Pencraft Book of the year 2021

CONTACT ME

I hope my books have added a little magick into your life. If you have a moment to add some to my day, you can help by telling your friends and leaving a review. Word-of-mouth is the most powerful way to share my stories. Thank you.

Love books? What about fun giveaways? Nope? Okay, can I entice you with underwater photos and cute dogs? Let's stay friends, receive my emails and contact me by signing up at my website

www.triciaomalley.com

Or find me on Facebook and Instagram.
@triciaomalleyauthor